Part I

For not an orphan in the wide world can be so
deserted as the child who is an outcast from a living
parent's love.

Charles Dickens

90710 000 522 634

Niki Mackay studied Performing Arts at the BRIT School, and it turned out she wasn't very good at acting but quite liked writing scripts. She holds a BA (Hons) in English Literature and Drama and won a full scholarship for her MA in Journalism.

Also by Niki Mackay

I, Witness

The Lies We Tell

Loaded

Taken

Niki Mackay

ORION

An Orion paperback

First published in Great Britain in 2022 by Orion Fiction,
an imprint of The Orion Publishing Group Ltd,
Carmelite House, 50 Victoria Embankment
London EC4Y 0DZ

An Hachette UK Company

1 3 5 7 9 10 8 6 4 2

A CIP catalogue record for this book is
available from the British Library.

ISBN (Mass Market Paperback) 978 1 4091 9528 3
ISBN (eBook) 978 1 4091 9529 0

Typeset by Input Data Services Ltd, Somerset

Printed in Great Britain by Clays Ltd, Elcograf S.p.A.

www.orionbooks.co.uk

For the Criminal Minds, writing can be a
lonely business but you make it less so

Chapter One

That night my mother wore a pencil dress with kitten heels in a powder blue and I was dressed to match. At fifteen, I was a pretty accessory for her to show off to her new friends. Or so I thought. In reality, I spent most of the evening standing around awkwardly in the shoes that pinched and a dress that seemed to make movement impossible. The party was in honour of my mother's engagement and upcoming wedding. It was the late sixties, the country was full of optimism and while the nation at large and the guests were swept up in a wave of joyous hope, I wasn't part of it and I couldn't have felt less like celebrating. I was largely ignored which was fine by me. Small talk wasn't something I was used to or particularly good at. My favourite conversations had been the ones I'd had with Daddy who was exhaustively interested in me, my views, what I thought, and what I was reading. An interest I'd taken for granted and missed sorely once it was gone.

Eventually I had slipped outside. There was nowhere in there to avoid the laughter and the music, and my room was being used for piles of guests' coats. I walked as far as our little summer house and sat in it. My back pressed to the cool wall and my eyes shut, remembering the day

I'd watched Daddy build this little place. My own outdoor playhouse. It seemed a hundred years ago, another lifetime and yet it had only been eight summers before. Mummy arguing that I was too old for such indulgence. Daddy knowing it would be a little wonderland where I'd take a book. I had never been more glad of it than after he'd gone. I'd sit in there surrounded by memories of him coming out and saying, 'Hey, kiddo.'

I was interrupted from my thoughts by a different voice: 'Penny for them.'

I found myself looking up at a very attractive young man. I had started to become interested in boys, of course, once I'd hit teenage years. At my all-girls school we had favourite pin-ups who we discussed endlessly between giggles, plans and hopes for future romances. I hadn't joined in these or many other conversations for a while by then but, for a moment looking up at that man's handsome face I was jolted back to some sort of teenage normality.

I think I blushed but murmured, 'It was a bit hot in there.'

He nodded and sat down next to me. I felt a little thrill at his closeness although I could also see stubble on his face and fine lines at the corners of his eyes. 'And bloody noisy, too, eh?'

I smiled, slightly shocked by his language and his inclusion of me, a child really, in it.

He looked at me narrow-eyed. 'Now you must be Nora's girl.'

'I am.'

'Even more beautiful than the bride-to-be.'

Bride-to-be.

I looked away. 'You're a friend of Harry's?' My uncle. Daddy's own brother and soon to be my step-father.

'Could say that. My dad used to deal with him. Business.' He waved a thinly fingered hand around.

'What do you do?'

'I'm in politics,' he grinned. 'For my sins. I went straight in out of university.'

'Oh wow.' And I meant it. Daddy had had high hopes for my ongoing education, and I was set to receive very good exam results. He'd been of the mind that I ought to do a few things before I settled down into family life. Getting educated was one of them and I'd continued to study hard even through the heartbreak of his loss because it's what he would have wanted.

'What was it like?'

He frowned. 'Politics?'

'University.'

He lit a cigarette, offering the pack to me which made me blush again. I shook my head.

'It was alright, more about the connections and whatnot, like school, eh?'

I nodded again as though I knew exactly what he was talking about, though I hadn't a clue. Most of the girls I knew were looking for marriage, but I had in mind that I'd like to study, and not secretarial college. I'd like a degree and Daddy had said why not. Other women were doing it after all.

The young man smoked for a bit, seemingly comfortable enough to sit in silence with a stranger. Everything about him spoke of ease. I knew from my mother what expensive clothes looked like; his suit was tailor made but he wore it casually. He had dirty blond hair, darker than mine and slightly long so that it fluttered around his very blue eyes.

He stubbed the cigarette out and said, 'Never mind all that, it's a party after all. I'm Jacob, Jacob Harse, and you are . . .?'

'Grace.'

'Lovely.' And he was looking at me very intently then. 'Lovely Grace.'

There was a silence. Long and stretching. His eyes seemed to turn a darker shade and he wobbled slightly as he adjusted himself on the thin bench of the summerhouse. I realised that he was probably quite drunk. Certainly, I could smell champagne on him and cigarettes and something else – a rich sort of sandalwood.

He was very close.

I said, 'I should probably get back.' And went to stand up.

He took my hand and grinned up at me. 'No rush though, eh?'

Without wishing to be impolite, something my mother and Harry had told me was an absolute no-no that evening, I sat next to him again.

When he leaned in to kiss me, I was so shocked I froze.

I was just fifteen. I'd never so much as held a boy's hand.

That night, Jacob Harse pressed me – a terrified young girl – down and took away something I hadn't been willing to give.

It couldn't have been a long time but it felt like the pain, the horror and the awful degradation lasted for hours. Afterwards he leapt to his feet, tidying himself up and offered me his hand, as though nothing out of the ordinary had occurred. I laid stock still where he'd pushed me to the ground. I could feel grass on my back, the little stumps that always grew between the wooden floorboards that my father had so carefully cut and laid. My dress was hitched up around my waist. Jacob shrugged. 'Suit yourself. And don't worry, I'll keep shtum about this, eh. Wouldn't want your reputation sullied.'

I didn't move, but I did feel tears running down my face and a wetness between my legs. I'd find out later it was mingled with blood which to my mind, as I sat in what was to become one of my regular scalding-hot baths, was indicative of the fact that I was broken in so many ways that night.

I didn't tell my mother. Didn't need to in the end. She noticed when I stopped using my sanitary products. She asked what had happened and I spoke in a rush of garbled words, not wanting her disapproval. Still clinging to the distant idea that she may come to my rescue. I spoke in brief, stilted, painful stops and starts, unable to meet her eye. Unsure if I'd be met with anger or disdain. What I got instead was a cold, detached indifference. Before Dad had died at least my basic needs were met by her. She cooked, cleaned, I was immaculately turned out. But, looking back I don't think she ever had much feeling for me one way or another. I've wondered since whether I myself was a means to an end. No other children came after me and she had been pregnant when they married. She was the reason I'd never met his parents, who'd disapproved, before they passed. I wondered how they would have felt knowing the girl they never liked married not one, but two of their sons.

With Daddy gone, our relationship, or lack thereof, was laid bare and clear. The neglect was no longer hidden nor counteracted by his love. She didn't lean over, as I'd hoped, and wrap me in her arms that day, she didn't tell me we'd make it right. The last glimmer of hope that she loved me evaporated and I knew loneliness then like few do. I wished desperately that I'd had siblings, or cousins. I wished for anyone other than her and dreadful Uncle Harry.

I told her what my rapist had said to me.

She nodded. 'Jacob is quite right – it will be your reputation that is harmed.'

I don't know what I had expected. But her voice was so flat, I could hardly bear it.

She told me, 'Life, Grace, isn't fair and looking back perhaps you've been far too protected from that.'

'You think this is my fault?'

'No. But it's you that it will impact.' She shrugged. 'I'll speak to Harry, we'll make a plan and this will all be over before you know it.'

Which was how I ended up at St Mary's home for unmarried mothers.

Chapter Two

It was a strange building. Grey, foreboding and steeped in all the trappings of religion. Everywhere you turned, pained saints looked down on you with condemning eyes and it was always freezing. Despite my pregnancy, the stress had made my appetite non-existent, and my thin limbs felt the cold. That sensation remained one of the strongest memories I had of St Mary's. Even when the sun shone on the fields surrounding it, inside it was frigid. The windows dripped with condensation and our breaths spilled out ahead of us in long chilly plumes.

My first night there was the first one I'd spent anywhere other than my own bed.

We arrived just before lunch.

We started out in the office, large and high ceilinged. Bare of decoration, it contained only the basics, which was how it was in every room of St Mary's. My head whirled with many things as a tight-lipped nun with a wide body spoke to my mother as though I wasn't in the room.

She left us alone for a moment and we said our awkward goodbyes. Me, hoping right until the very last second that my mother would step forward and grasp me in her arms. But she left with a nod and a perfunctory goodbye.

She didn't reach out to me. She didn't touch me. I sat in that front office watching through the large windows as my mother walked away and into the car with Harry. She didn't look back.

The nun, Sister Marjorie, came back and said, 'I'll take you up then.'

I followed her, accompanied by the persistent feeling of nausea that reminded me even in the tiny seconds where I might be able to forget that my body was housing someone else. An unasked for, unwanted invader. I wondered if this was how my own mother had felt.

I was six months gone by the time I arrived there. My belly was small still but definitely starting to protrude, and I swayed softly from side to side with each step.

We got to a large room with six beds in threes and the nun told me to put my things in the drawers next to the one that was to be mine. As I did, she talked me through the daily schedule, which seemed to be mostly chores and religious instruction. She said on Sundays we went to church.

I had made it just in time for lunch and after I'd put my meagre possessions in the drawer, I followed her down to a dining hall filled with raucous noise which was quelled as we stepped in.

There were lots of girls there, some older than me or near my age, and they all stopped mid-conversation and stood abruptly, saying, 'Hello, Sister Marjorie' in unison.

She nodded at them and said, 'This is Grace.' No one said anything. I felt heat rise in my face.

The nun snapped her fingers. 'Agnes, show her where to get lunch.'

Agnes was tall, towering over me by a long stretch. She had fierce red skin that looked sore and dark eyes. She smiled sweetly at the nun and said, 'Yes, Sister.'

After 'Sister' left she turned to me, pointed at the table at the back, and said, 'Horrible stew, help yerself.'

'Thank you very much.'

She stared and then she burst out laughing. I had no idea what I'd said that was funny but a few of the other girls stood up and came over to stand next to her. She nudged one who had sharp pointed features then said to me, 'Say again.'

Not knowing what else to do, I said, 'Thank you very much,' as if it was a question.

That laughter came, this time with the girls either side of her joining in. My face flushed and I took a step forward. I was surprised to find I was hungry and figured I'd eat, then try to get away. Agnes sidestepped so her thick and very pregnant body blocked me. I went the other way and so did she. That's when I felt the first stirrings of fear.

At my school there was the odd spat, but we were nice girls from nice families. We fought with our words, not our fists. I had a glimmer that that wouldn't be the case here. These girls were what my mother would call rough.

At home there hadn't been violence either, aside from Jacob Harse, but I felt the threat of it then.

My heart hammered in my chest and one hand went reflexively to my stomach, cupping the unwanted child within.

I said, 'Excuse me.'

And all amusement vanished from Agnes's face. It

scrunched in on itself, lip raising in a sneer. 'Check out la-de-da here.'

Her friends murmured in agreement, of what I didn't know, but I did know that every eye in that dining hall was turned on me and something inside registered that the way I dealt with this would have a direct impact on how things went for me there. This terrible place that I was to be stuck in for the foreseeable future. I felt a wave of anger. They were laughing at my voice, because I spoke well. Something I couldn't help. Any more than I could help Daddy dying or Mummy marrying Harry or Jacob doing this to me. I didn't want to be there and it wasn't my fault that I was.

I looked at her and said, 'Get out of my way.'

Her eyes narrowed, one hand curling up in between us and making a fist. 'Come on then.'

And so I had my first fight.

I don't remember much about it other than every single frustration of the awful years that had come before that day seemed to come out of me through my hands and I went for it. I know she landed more than one heavy-handed punch on me, smacks that turned into florid bruises afterwards; at the time, though, I felt nothing.

And I kept going until I felt several pairs of hands lifting me up. I was moved away and backwards, shocked to see Agnes on the floor cowering at my feet, her nose bloodied and her eyes wide with fright.

I felt a sharp slap to the back of my head and that one did register. I turned and faced the sister who'd booked me in. She said, 'I expected better from a girl from your walk of life – fancy starting fights on your first day here.' She tutted. I stood panting from the exertion, stunned by the whole thing.

Someone said, 'Agnes started it,' as Agnes herself got to her feet. I was ashamed by the state of her until I realised that my own lip was bleeding, and that voice was right. I hadn't started this.

Sister Marjorie turned to Agnes, 'Is this so?'

Agnes mumbled something and the voice piped up again, 'Bullies hate getting what for, eh?' The owner of the voice stood. She was very striking looking with a round babyish face, long auburn hair, bright blue eyes, and a smattering of freckles on pale skin. She smiled at me and said to the nun, 'I'll take the new girl and clean her up. Maybe just let it all cool down. I'm sure Agnes won't be causing any more dramas, will you, Ag?'

Agnes nodded but grumpily and I had a sudden urge to laugh at the absurdity of it all.

The nun said, 'Very well and I expect no more of this.'

Chapter Three

It wasn't that Lola Scott-Tyler was heroic, she just didn't like bullies. Plus, she respected that the girl had stuck up for herself. She'd looked at her and written her off so was surprised to see her not only lose her rag with dreadful Agnes but properly lay into her too. If nothing else it broke up the boredom a bit.

She didn't want to be here any more than any of the other girls did. She was still pretty livid at having been sent away and she was also heartbroken at being apart from the man she was in love with. The one she could never have, not properly anyway, though knowing he adored her and was missing her was enough. She'd managed to phone him once from a phone box on one of their awful walks into town. He'd not been happy to hear from her at first but, although he said she wasn't to risk it again, he also said he loved her and that was like a balm to Lola.

She'd known her dad would be furious when he found out about the baby. She was fifteen, not even able to get married legally, and worse still, had refused to give up the father's name so there was no chance of menacing the poor bugger into a shotgun wedding as soon as she turned sixteen either – though in fairness if her dad knew who it was he wouldn't be arranging a party, he'd be committing murder. She'd expected to be able to stay home and front it out instead and Lola was used to getting her own way.

She pushed it from her mind, then linked arms with the new girl and they walked towards the dorm. In the awful bathroom Lola helped her clean up. The girl stayed silent. The only sound was Lola running water and Grace's uneven breathing. Adrenaline. Lola knew it well; explosive violence and flared tempers were an everyday part of her world, though she herself was never on the receiving end of such things. Everyone knew who her dad was and therefore no one would dare mess with Lola. But she'd been witness to it. Felt the threat of it on the streets where they lived and saw the impact of it on neighbours and friends. Poverty, she always thought, was like cancer, and though money wasn't a concern for her family now, it was for their wider community. She didn't think it was the same for the well-spoken, nicely dressed girl she was dabbing at with a wet cloth, but you never knew of course. Girls like her really had no place being somewhere like this, yet here she was.

'Don't talk much, do you?'

Grace shrugged but her breath was steadier, her shoulders dropping ever so slightly.

'Good to see Agnes get what for though.'

'I didn't start it.'

Lola grinned. ''Course you didn't. Agnes is a bully is all, took you for weaker and thought she'd have a prod at you. It's your voice, mate, that annoyed her, and your pretty face.'

Grace looked out the window. 'Fat lot of good it's done

me so far.' And she sounded so sad that Lola felt a wave of sympathy and the urge to protect her.

'Still better than looking like Agnes.' And she pulled a face that finally drew a smile.

Chapter Four

Something good grew, even in that awful place where boredom was like an incessant disease. I laughed and joked with Lola. As our bellies enlarged so did the words between us. She asked me about my parents, I told her about my dad dying, Mum and Harry getting married. I also told her that the man who'd done this to me was a friend of theirs.

She put her long arm around me, pulling my body close to hers and resting her chin on my head, and she said, 'That's utter shit.'

After that night we got into each other's beds after lights out, our ridiculous stomachs pressing around for space in the tiny, cramped cots, but as Lola said, better than freezing yer knackers off. One of those night she woke me and I turned to her.

She said, 'The little'un's coming.'

My first thought was a selfish one. She'd be leaving first and the thought of being here without her was unbearable.

She said, 'Help me up to Matron.'

I did and sat outside listening to her wails and moans.

Eventually, Sister Marjorie came out and saw me sitting there in the corridor, and said, 'She's asking for you.' In a stern voice and then with a sigh, she added, 'You may as well go, say your goodbyes.'

I stepped in. There was a strange smell in there. The copper of blood and something else. Earthy and indefinable. Lola looked pale and tired, and I said as much. She smiled faintly and said, 'You wait.'

Then seeing the terror on my face, she reached for my hand.

'You'll be fine. You're a strong one. Just like me.'

I nodded, hand under my belly. Any day now.

I said, 'You're leaving?'

She nodded. 'I will be.' She squeezed my hand. Then, 'Pass my bag up.' Matron had packed her things and I reached for them. She took out a small pad and a pencil. Handed me a London address. 'If you ever need me . . .'

I nodded but knew that the chances of us ever meeting again were very slim. I'd never have known anyone like her, our paths wouldn't have crossed if things had been anything close to normal. 'Grace.'

I met her eyes, desperately trying to keep the tears from mine.

She pulled me to her, and I clung then. Inhaling the now familiar smell of her, ripe that day with something else.

She said, 'If you ever need me.' Again.

And I nodded. 'It'll be rubbish here without you.'

She grinned, put a hand on my stomach. 'It won't be long.'

I said, 'I'll miss you.'

'I'll miss you too.'

And then Sister Marjorie was there, ushering me away.

That night I put her address in the inside zip of my own case.

Lola was right though – I didn't have long there without her. The following evening my baby girl arrived.

Chapter Five

Lola was sore when she got home and knackered. She'd been more than happy to see her mum, Mae, at St Mary's and had handed the baby straight over. Now she was back in the smoke, had eaten a decent meal and put away three cups of sugary tea all with her feet up. Everyone was home, and a fair amount of fuss was being made over the baby. Sam, Mae had decided to call him, and while Lola had definitely felt a wave of love for him, she was very glad he'd be her little brother, not her son and that Mae would see to the boy's day-to-day needs. She understood she was meant to keep a low profile for a bit. She'd do it, had to swallow it obviously but she thought her parents were ridiculous. Anyone with half a brain could work out the new baby was hers and not Mae's but she also knew that no one would dare say anything about it. In fairness, her mum would do a much better job than she ever could.

She'd missed this place and her mum's fussing. Even now with a little one in her arms she was in and out of the living room, bringing whisky in for her dad and brother, another hot sweet tea for Lola which she sipped gratefully. Birthing wasn't for wusses, it turned out, and she honestly didn't think she ever wanted to repeat the experience. Marvelled at the fact her mother had done it twice and plenty of women they knew many more times than that. Hardly seemed worth the hassle for what was over in a few minutes anyway. All that aside she wanted to see her man again sooner rather than later. Not for that. All Lola wanted from him was a cuddle, maybe a good cry on his shoulder. She was good at keeping things together, made a point of trying not to let things bother her. Happy-go-lucky, that's how she was thought of, how her family, friends and community saw her, and for the most part she was. Maybe it was the birth. Or the time away from home, the first in her life, but she felt fragile. Exhausted from it all and from also not being able to speak the truth. She'd almost told Grace, had wanted to and instinctively known her new friend would be a good ear, but she'd promised him silence and her word mattered. She'd learnt that well enough over the years.

Her dad sank down next to her, arm across her shoulders and gave her a quick squeeze. 'Alright, girl?'

'I am, yeah.'

He nodded. 'Good.' She inhaled the smell of him. Cigars and whisky. Tears sprang into her eyes. She was forgiven and she was relieved. Though she was rarely on the receiving end of his temper it was an awful thing when it exploded. He had been apoplectic over this and if he ever found out the truth the ramifications would be awful for them all.

She was glad to see him take Sam from her mum and look down at the baby with a gentle grin. He was a known face around here, owned among other things a pub, a betting shop and a boxing gym. None of which, she understood, would have been easy to come by for a boy born into London's slums. He'd fought for what he had and fought hard. She knew he had a reputation for things she preferred not to dwell on. For all that, when it came to his family, Daniel Scott-Tyler was like butter. He'd look after and provide for the baby just as he had Lola and River. She felt an unexpected wave of jealousy towards her newborn son. A confusing feeling and it passed as fast as it had arrived. But it gave her pause. She was jealous of his innocence, she supposed, and that chance to start over. Mae and Daniel were good parents, she knew that, and now they were his parents, and he was little and cute and had never done anything wrong. He wasn't having to go about life holding in a dark secret that would tear them all apart.

Mae said, 'You OK, love?'

She forced herself to smile at her mother and blinked away her unshed tears. 'Tired.'

Mae nodded. 'Women's work'll do that to a body. They've no idea, these men.' Daniel rolled his eyes and Lola smiled for real then.

She thought about Grace. Whether she'd had her baby and how she'd coped with the whole thing. Her first girl-friend, Grace was. Lola had always been more of a tomboy, running about with her skirts hitched and biking down steep hills, fearless with her brother whom she adored. Her parents thought she was too in with her male counterparts but there was nothing like that in it – they were her pals, was all. Her unlikely friendship at St Mary's had distracted her from all of that for a bit. Stopped her missing him and wondering. Grace was so deeply, unequivocally sad. What had happened to her was awful and Lola couldn't imagine a mother so cold or what it must be like to be so utterly alone, although right now she wouldn't mind five minutes to have a cry in peace, put to bed her confused, mangled feelings once and for all. Daniel squeezed her shoulder again and she leaned into him, shutting her eyes.

The door went and they all looked at each other. Daniel frowned, the baby still in his arms. He went to stand, and Mae waved him back down, going to the door herself.

They all heard the sounds of a woman crying. Lola whispered, 'That's Gladys.'

Daniel rolled his eyes. 'Probably off her head and looking for money.'

Lola nodded, not pointing out that Mae would likely bung her a few coins then lie to Daniel about it. Gladys Simpson was a nightmare. She'd been on the game for years and had a string of so many kids they all lost count. Four, Lola thought, she'd given birth four times. All different dads, too, as far as anyone could tell, occupational hazard for her. No wonder she was off her head all the time. According to Mae, who'd caught Lola up on all the local gossip as Dan drove them back from St Mary's, Gladys had recently descended so far into her cups that the woman rarely drew a sober breath.

Mae poked her head around the door now, a worried look on her face. 'It's young Benjamin – he's not come home.'

Daniel frowned. 'Which one's he?'

'The little one, the youngest boy, and not even ten yet.'

Daniel smirked. 'If I was one of her kids I wouldn't come home either.'

'Daniel.' Mae's heart was racing and she wasn't in the mood for jokes from him.

He looked back down at Sam then his daughter, sheepish now, 'Sorry. But I'm sure he's fine.'

Mae was wriggling into her coat. 'You're likely right. I'm going to go help Gladys look anyway. Alright?'

'Yeah, OK. River, go give them a hand.' He'd just come into the room with a steaming cup of tea, which he now put down next to his dad with a sigh. 'Come on then, Mum.'

Chapter Six

The day that I gave birth to my daughter, Chloe McCain, remains the best and worst of my life.

I had had no real expectations of the event itself further than a sense of fear, which proved to be perfectly reasonable. The birthing room was above our dorms and so we all heard the terrible noises that came from there, but no one explained what was going to happen.

It was a cruel oversight and I wondered, in later years, whether some of the sterner nuns had used the growing fear and trepidation as a form of punishment and penance. Like being marched through town every Sunday morning in a shameful line to church while the locals looked on at our obvious predicaments. The sixties were revolutionary, looking back, but real tangible change was slow, and the world was an unforgiving time for mothers with no husbands. No one cared how you'd got there; it was always an unforgiving time. I'm not sure honestly how much better things have got but back then the animosity was open and encouraged. It worked too. On top of the terrible feelings I already had about myself, a new shame took hold. Only Lola seemed unaffected, smiling and nodding at parishioners who turned to look away during service. I even saw her wink at some of the men more than once and certainly when the sister saw she'd have her knuckles rapped for it. I felt stronger in her presence. Buoyed by her boldness. When I asked her one night if the shame ever got to her, she'd laughed. 'Don't see the dads being frog-marched on parade, do ya?'

And I thought about that, about how I'd got there. About Jacob Harse studying, a bright future already mapped out for him in the way that privilege takes care of itself. I suspected I wasn't the only girl placed in St Mary's after rape. Even the babies arriving out of consensual couplings hadn't put themselves in the womb. I developed a fierce sense of the unfairness and eventually I stopped walking with my head down and glared at the people who stared at us. If only they knew. If only they cared.

The pain of childbirth was intense, worsened by a series of terrible complications, which at various points endangered my life and hers. The nuns in the room, Sister Marjorie in particular, kept me going through agony so terrible I thought I might die, and that it may even be preferable to what I was experiencing then.

It was with great surprise then, when I was handed a shrivelled little girl in a soft holey blanket to feed, that I had it in me to feel the most acute and perfect love.

I was ripped to shreds, burning a fever and in a serious condition but all of that paled when I held the tiny thing I'd never wanted.

I fed her and for half an hour, while we waited for the doctor who was to sew me up and declare that I'd never bear any more children, I felt a real unexpected peace.

I sank in and out of consciousness over the next few days. Chloe was brought to me for feeding and taken away again in between.

For six short and wonderful weeks I nursed her, changed her, fed her and bathed her. I was the only one on the ward. Chloe and I had the place to ourselves. As my body knitted back together slowly, my heart became full of love for her.

Eventually, at the start of the fifth week since Chloe's birth, I asked Sister Marjorie what would happen now, half-knowing and very much not wanting the answer.

She said a family had been found for Chloe.

I broke then. I sobbed and sobbed, the baby clutched to me as Sister Marjorie sat beside me, her sturdy arm draped over my shoulders. I begged to keep my little girl.

In the end she patted my hand and said, 'Let's meet with your mother, and we'll have a chat, yes?'

I didn't know what that meant, but it wasn't a no.

Chapter Seven

No one found Benjamin that night, nor the next day nor the one after that. The police looked for a short period then shrugged their shoulders. Likely the boy had had an accident, maybe fallen into the Thames. He wasn't well supervised after all, everyone knew that. Mum on the bash and half-pissed most days, and none of them knew who their dads were. The whole family was in such a mess that it was astonishing that greater tragedy hadn't befallen Gladys and her brood already, though no one could call any of their lives easy.

Byron, the eldest, had always kept a close eye on his siblings, including the younger boy. He was sixteen and strong. He used that, waiting each day at the docks for work as it came in, trying to bring in some money for the younger ones and so that his mum didn't have to do what it was she did. His main problem, though, the thing that went against him time and time again, was the colour of his skin. People were racist and Byron, who was of mixed heritage, bore the brunt of it. It was sad but true and like so much in his life it wasn't fair.

Gladys became more of a disaster than she'd already been in the days, weeks and months that followed Benjamin's disappearance. Byron was devastated and felt truly old before his years. On top of his grief was the very real worry that he wouldn't be able to bring in enough to feed them anymore, let alone pay the rent on the shithole they were cramped into. Thing was, no one else would let to them, a mixed bag ragtag crew. No dad, Gladys so obviously incapable. If they lost this place, hovel though it was, they'd be in even more dire straits. A roof was a roof after all. Four damp walls were a step up from no walls.

He did his best, keeping his two remaining siblings fed, trying to remind them they were loved, if not always cared for. And all the while missing the little boy so much his heart ached. He was the best of them, Benjamin, a lovely looking little lad but with too trusting a nature. Byron sat up in the small hours wondering if that had been half the problem. They all doted on Ben, even Rita who was actually a year younger than him. He was so childlike, so cheerful even in the face of all the adversity they faced. Maybe trying to protect the boy from the very real horrors of their lives had been a mistake. Byron could imagine Benjamin being charmed by anyone, being taking off, being led to . . . God knew what. Or maybe, like the police said, he'd had an accident, though to Byron that seemed unlikely. Kids here played out in huge half-feral packs. They roamed the city and were savvy in that way. Whatever the cause, his brother wasn't there. His mother was a hysterical mess, and his two younger siblings, Goldie and Rita, were looking to him for guidance and care he wasn't sure he could give.

Everyone in that area felt the ripple effects of it. They'd all had a lot to say about Gladys, of course, but no one wished harm on a little one and they all felt the fear of it. A child, one of their own, disappeared into thin air like that. How could a little boy just vanish? While what everyone was saying was, of course, right – Gladys didn't look after the lad – it was still a tragedy. But she loved the kids in her own haphazard way and besides, no one deserved this.

It was a close-knit community and the Scott-Tyler's were at the very heart of it. Mae was as upset as if it had been one of her own. She went round that first day with dinner for the family and her heart broke at what she saw there. Three kids, as they were now minus Benjamin, cramped into three rooms. The state of each one was awful. She felt a wave of shame. There she was with her lot and more space than she needed, house beautifully decorated. Even the whole thing with Lola had turned out OK. She never found mothering difficult, especially when they were small and you were their whole world. She had been scathing about Gladys's parenting skills, of course, and had found herself annoyed by her over the years, not least when she'd moved onto the same road as them. They all had. She'd also partaken in some sharp and barbed gossip, which she found herself ashamed about as she stood there in front of the older boy who had answered the door. She saw him stick his chin out and felt the embarrassment for him acutely. This was no way to live, and he knew it. She'd seen him on her morning walks waiting for work. He was big, strong, and more than anything else, she realised, he was hungry. Not unlike her Dan had been back in the day; a boy like that should go far, but his skin would go against him and she imagined he only ever got work when everyone else had turned it down. He could be her boy, River, if things were different. She'd married a good man, one of the best, and she and Daniel were a formidable team. But that was luck as much as anything else. Gladys had been put on the game by Byron's dad, a terrible man they all knew by reputation, and she'd been young then. A girl really, he'd left her high and dry with Byron and the boy's sister, Goldie. Would she herself have managed any better than Gladys had? She'd never had to find out, luckily.

Mae said, 'I've brought food and come to see your mum's alright.'

He still stood rigid and hard. She didn't move, and in the end she smiled at him, and he moved aside with a sigh.

She stepped in, forcing herself not to wince at the wretched odours in the place. 'Come on, love, let me help out. Where shall I put this?' She ended up serving it in three chipped bowls to Byron and his siblings. Gladys was in bed when Mae went through to the woman. She was out of it, her emaciated face tear-stained, a bottle next to her bed while the little ones contended with empty cupboards and bellies. Something had to be done. She knew that and Mae being Mae, wouldn't be leaving it up to someone else.

It was her urging that sent Daniel round offering the eldest lad work.

Chapter Eight

A week later my mother arrived, with Harry 'in the car outside'.

I held out the baby to her as Sister had suggested I do. She was newly cleaned, her fair hair fluffy around her tiny head, and dressed in a pink dress, her small, chicken-thin legs sticking out at sideways angles, sleeping calmly. Angelic she was and my mother didn't even look. Sister Marjorie gestured for her to sit.

I adjusted myself sorely and carefully, covering Chloe again and clutching the bundle of blankets that held my calm and pretty child.

My mother was the first to speak, 'Why is the baby here?'

Sister Marjorie said, 'We have a family for her.' And as I started to protest, she put up a hand to silence me. My mother still didn't even glance my way.

'Now, when Grace birthed her there were some complications.' She looked at me and gave one of her rare smiles. 'She did very well but sadly the baby . . .'

'Chloe,' I said.

'Chloe will be the only child that she will ever have.'

My mother didn't respond, but started to stand. 'And now would be the time for your goodbyes.'

I remained frozen to the spot. Chloe's little legs wriggled within my arms. She'd be due a feed soon. The plan now was for bottles, but my bound chest flooded with milk for her.

Sister Marjorie said to my mother, 'Perhaps you might consider taking your daughter, and granddaughter home. To avoid any shame, you could say you'd adopted a child in need . . .'

My mother frowned. 'Absolutely not. This has all been a terrible mistake and one that we'll be able to put behind us now.'

I was crying, hot, awful tears.

My mother looked at me then Sister Marjorie. 'We have paid you and paid you well. My husband has made a size-able donation to your trust. We did so to ensure this,' she gestured towards me, 'was taken care of. Now I walk in here and find myself barraged with all sorts of nonsense.'

Chloe had started to cry. My mother flinched at the sound.

'I'll wait outside. Grace, your bag in the car.'

And she turned and left.

Sister Marjorie's face was as stricken as my heart felt.

I said, 'She's hungry,' in a voice that sounded strangled and desperate. Thick with my grief and horror.

Sister stood, pressed a hand on my shoulder and said, 'Child, why don't you feed her?'

I nourished my baby through the pain of what I would discover was mastitis, but worse by far was the agony of my broken heart. Sister left me for a moment. I was to find out many years later that she had gone outside and again pleaded my case to my mother and Harry. Her pleas fell on deaf ears.

She came back in a mere twenty minutes later. Chloe was full and asleep again. I held her pressed to me, trying desperately to memorise the feel of her there.

Sister took her from me gently and as she left the room, I screamed and screamed until she came back in with Matron in tow, her mouth set in a grim, determined line and a needle in her hand.

The next thing I knew I was being shaken awake by Harry.

'We're home,' he said, not looking me in the eye.

I was laid across the back seat of his car and as my body wakened from a drug-induced slumber, various parts of me burned with pain and the memory of the daughter I'd lost.

I stepped from the car on cotton wool legs and sank quickly to my knees on our pebble-stoned drive. I heard my mother mutter, 'For goodness' sake.' And Harry picked me up, carrying me inside as I drifted away again into sleep.

I woke with a start in a dark room and simultaneously pressed one hand to my belly and reached one out for Lola. My hand met a gelatinous mess where there had so recently been a firm life-filled bump and Lola wasn't there. Inside my dress, which I was still wearing, I found the thin nursing cloth. I had been using it to feed Chloe, catching the trickles of my milk that escaped from her little mouth down my body. I pressed it to my face, overwhelmed by the smell of her and me mingled.

Everything came back including the soreness that birth

had brought and the far worse pain as Sister had pulled her away from me. My chest ached and leaked, the bruising between my legs was still tender weeks on and my insides felt shredded. But I relished it. It was, after all, everything I had left of her.

It was dark in the bedroom that had always been mine and no longer felt like home. Without my father there it was just a house. A strange and foreign place. One where I was no longer welcome.

St Mary's was hardly a holiday but between Lola and Sister Marjorie with her stern face and soft heart I'd found more love there than what was left for me here.

It smelled different. My sheets were fresh and ironed, the bed undeniably more comfortable than the one I'd been sleeping in for so many nights. But still I longed to be back there.

I shut my eyes again, but sleep eluded me. I was exhausted, inside and out, but every time I drifted off, I thought I heard her croaky, hungry cry and woke up to wet parches on my chest, her little cloth pressed against my face and the awfulness of my empty arms.

Chapter Nine

Samuel had the temperament of his mother, but Mae somehow found it easier to deal with in a boy. Mae had a little brother but she wasn't in contact with him by then and she didn't dwell on that. She'd had to choose between her birth family and her husband and she'd made that choice knowing the consequences, but when he'd been a baby she was besotted by him and wondered if that's why she felt more drawn to River and protective towards him. She'd never say it aloud, of course, and she adored her daughter but she'd always favoured River, just as she suspected Daniel had always favoured Lola. He was much more lenient with her anyway. River was easy to like, charming and pleasant. He always had been.

Now she had that same soft feeling towards Sam, who was slowly wrapping her and everyone else around his pudgy little baby finger. For Lola's part she'd behaved well since she got home and helped out with the baby when asked. She loved him as she would have a little brother and that was as it should be and absolutely fine as far as Mae was concerned. Plus, Daniel had taken an unexpected shine to the little fella. He was home earlier and more often, and that meant River was too. They were all sitting down for dinners together at the table of an evening. Often with Byron, Goldie and Rita in attendance too. Dan had taken Byron on because his wife had made him, for no other reason, and he'd done so with trepidation as well. He didn't give a toss where the lad's lineage came from or how he looked, but he'd understood a few of the old boys on his firm would have something to say about it. As it turned out, Byron was such a good worker, keen, hungry, desperate to get ahead, that those old boys could do one as far as Dan was concerned.

Byron did what he was asked to do, quietly and without fuss. He was respectful, discreet and an asset. To be honest he reminded Dan of himself at the same age. He and his best friend Big Des had formed what was referred to back then as an 'unholy alliance'. That made him smile even now.

They'd been a couple of terrors in their day, that was for sure, but they were single-minded. They'd both grown up without a pot to piss in. Knew what it was like to be raised with bugger all and they both wanted more. Now they had it. Byron understood that in a way River never could. Wasn't the boy's fault, of course, and the fact that he hadn't had to struggle was a point of honour for Daniel. He provided in a way his useless dad never had. Byron's siblings were actually very sweet girls, too, and he knew Mae was back and forth over the road helping the girls to try to spruce the place up. A hopeless project really and he was toying with the idea of giving Byron a deposit to rent somewhere better. If he carried on calling in old debts and settling old scores so well, he would.

Terrible business with the boy, of course, which Dan tried not to think about. But it had also changed that family's fortunes and as usual Daniel was very happy to be a part of a good-news story.

Mae put plates of food on the table, slapping Lola's hand away when she reached for a potato. He winked at his daughter, and she smiled back. The baby yelled, 'Lola' and she rolled her eyes but took his little hand in hers.

Daniel had been heartbroken when she'd told them about the baby and he still wasn't happy that she wouldn't give him a name for the father, but he wouldn't be without the boy now.

Funny how things turned out sometimes.

A year ago, when Lola was due to return home, he'd still been in his anger. Mae had done her best to calm him down as she always did but the months Lola had been away were terrible. He knew young girls who got in trouble, saw it all the time in his walk of life, but he could have guessed their paths at three, four, five. They ran away from awful, troubled situations, then bam — a belly full of arms and legs before they were grown. He'd expected better for his girl. That's what stung. He'd honestly not been convinced he'd get over it, had even talked to Mae about having the baby adopted. Mae had been horrified and while he got his way in sending Lola off — more so that he didn't have to see her pregnant than for appearance's sake — no one was fooled: his wife would not even entertain the idea of not taking in their own flesh and blood.

Now the child was here he couldn't believe he'd considered it. But there you go. Lola was behaving at least. He saw that Byron was single and wondered if that might be encouraged. He wouldn't be averse to having the lad in the family proper. Honestly, he was starting to rely more on him than River. River was a good boy, naturally likable and charming, but he didn't really do thinking on his own. In fairness it had never been something Daniel encouraged. Byron had had trouble settling a debt a few weeks ago and instead of running in roughshod, he'd sorted out a payment plan. It had meant Daniel got some of the money up front, so wasn't having the piss taken, he knew the chances of getting the rest were good and he'd come out of it looking like a hero. River would have just smashed the bloke up, which was how they usually did things. Byron had smoother ways and an innate sense of fairness that Daniel admired.

Mae pressed a hand on his shoulder and swung down to kiss his cheek. Her red hair fell like a curtain around them, and he felt the same swell of love he always did around his wife.

'You alright, love?'

He grinned. 'I really am, Mae, you?'

'More than.' She sat down at their crowded table. The only person missing from the Scott-Tyler or the Simpson families was Gladys. She'd been seen out at the Wheelwright Arms two days ago. Byron had made the mistake of handing her half his pay cheque. The boy had a blind spot when it came to that woman, but Daniel suspected he wouldn't make the same mistake twice.

Benjamin, of course, was also absent and despite the buoyant mood and the obvious improvement for his siblings, his absence weighed heavy in Byron's heart. He'd resigned himself by now to the fact that no good had come to his baby brother. Most likely someone knew where he was and who was responsible, so he kept an ear out for any information. One day he'd find out who it was and then he'd kill them.

Chapter Ten

Months passed by and turned into a year. I turned sixteen. My body healed, piecing itself back together as best it could, but my heart never did. Always there would be a sore spot. A place of excruciating agony that I could ill afford to visit. In the daytime I tried only to think of what I was doing at that moment. If thoughts of Daddy, Jacob or Chloe drifted into my mind I pushed them away. I visualised them as physical things, shunting them out of my mind like black smoke rising.

But in the night when my brain rested I couldn't trick it and I would be caught unaware sleeping – the defences of my conscious mind down. For years to come I was to wake, panicked, covered in sweat with my heart beaten to a pulp.

I became harder.

Certainly, I no longer fitted in with the girls in my class though I carried on doing far better than they did in tests despite the missed months. Not that that even mattered. Much of our learning by then was how to run a house, cook dinner and be a good wife. A future no longer inevitable for me. I wouldn't be having a family, so what was the point in a husband? My assumed plans that I would marry well were in tatters. Who'd want me?

Besides, after Jacob I couldn't imagine myself ever wanting to be touched by a man. I didn't do the things I used to either, like encouraging my classmates or helping with homework, and they began to draw away from me. That cheerful Grace, bombing around class without a care in the world, was a ghost now. Some former version of myself that I hardly recognised.

They talked about me, the other girls, in small whispers, or aloud when they thought I was out of earshot.

Rumours spread and the obvious conclusion was finally grasped at. I didn't deny anything. I didn't engage in conversation at all. I found I honestly didn't care what they said – what were words, after all, in the grand scheme of things? My mother seemed to say something hurtful at least once a day if she spoke to me at all, and eventually I tuned her out too. Everything became background noise as I trudged through my life as if I was wading through treacle.

I went to my classes. I read the set texts, figured out the maths equations, cooked 'family dinners' and learnt to iron men's shirts and bedsheets. I eventually sat my exams and left each one certain I was close to one hundred percent. If I let myself daydream at all it would be Daddy and me opening my results, him hugging me to him and telling me how proud he was. But that reality never came to pass and just thinking about it brought tears to my eyes. How quickly life could change.

My mother implied that finding myself work and moving on wouldn't be such a bad idea. In her words, 'How much more could you learn from books?' The careful dreams Daddy had made me think were mine finally slipped away into a distant impossibility. I wasn't going to keep studying, I wasn't going to have a wonderful career and get married to some fine fellow. I was never going to have the children I'd dreamed of raising.

I was on my own.

I scoured papers for live-in jobs and tried to imagine my life as a maid or a cook or a housekeeper. It was with a cutting humour that I considered all the lessons I'd thought of as a waste of time were likely to be the only ones I'd have any use for now. What else was there for an unmarried woman with no family to support her? Even secretarial college, which I'd once sneered at, was outside of my grasp.

One night when I was searching through the classifieds, honestly certain that things couldn't get any worse, I was proved wrong once again.

There was yet another party at ours. It was hours past midnight when the music finally turned off and people started to leave. Eventually there was just the low murmur of voices in the garden. The tinkle of my mother's laugh and Harry's guffaw.

Then I heard a braying tone that chilled my blood.

No.

It couldn't be.

My mother had no love for me, God knows I knew that by then.

But this was low. Unthinkable. It couldn't be so.

I crept to the top of the stairs, listening.

It was him. I could never forget his voice, any more than I could forget the feel of his hands on me.

I felt like I was walking in some kind of dream state, as though I was treading not on the lovely, carpeted landing and the floorboards of my pretty pink bedroom, but on cotton wool instead. I went back to my room, dressed quickly and pulled the little red suitcase last used for St Mary's out from underneath my bed. I packed some clothes, a picture of Daddy and me, and Chloe's blanket, my hand running across the inside pocket searching for the address Lola had given me. Then I crept down the stairs.

They kept cash in the house. Harry loved to carry it around in big obscene wedges. I'd watched Mother pout at him for the things she wanted and him reach up high for the hidden tin, licking his thumb and peeling notes from the fat little packages.

I had to move a chair to reach it, which I did as quietly as I could.

I found the box and was relieved when I opened it and found it stuffed full of cash.

I took all of the money, then pressed the lid of the tin down gently and put it back empty in the cupboard, aware of every sound I made, focused finally on the loudness of the zipper of the inside pocket and the clunk of the locks as I fastened my bag having placed the cash securely inside.

So focused was I, that I didn't hear anyone come in behind me and when a voice said, 'Oh now, lovely Gracie,' I jumped and turned. A deer frozen in the terrible headlights of his gaze.

He looked just the same, floppy hair still grazing his eyebrows, grin in place and that sense of ease.

I was glued to the spot. There was so much I wanted to

say but I knew that none of it mattered, not to him. Not to my mother, not to Harry.

I wanted to tell him about her, my baby, with her skin so smooth it was like stroking velvet. The way one eyebrow rose when she was nearing the end of a feed.

I don't know why I didn't consider this awful man her father. She was mine. Even though she had been wrenched from me and given to other people, that would never change. I suppose I wanted him to feel some sorrow for her, at what had been perfect and now was lost.

He took steps into the kitchen, reaching casually across me for a bottle on the side. He waved it at me, and I noticed his wedding ring glinting on his finger. He said, 'Nightcap?'

I didn't say anything and he laughed.

He leant down, rummaging around in a cupboard. Looking for a glass, I suppose.

My eyes went to the door, and I stooped to pick up my suitcase. He banged his head on the top of the inside of the cupboard and muttered, 'Blast.'

Drunk again.

My fingers moved along the work surface, my eyes fixed on what I was reaching for. It was as if my body was one step ahead of my mind and it was something of a surprise when my fingers picked up the shiny knife sitting next to a half-cut lemon and plunged it into Jacob's back.

He made a high-pitched sound, somewhere between a wail and a scream, and his body tilted forward, head smashing again against the cabinet. No 'Blast' this time and for some reason that made me smile.

Then he seemed to curl into himself and was crawling on all fours. There was no blood for what felt like ages but was probably just seconds, then it came and as he levered himself around on all fours, he left a trail of it.

He was yelling now, 'Help, help.' The knife wobbled from his back like a shark's fin bobbing over the waves of the sea. His voice pulled me from my dark reverie.

I picked up my suitcase, turned and walked out of the kitchen just as my mother and Harry came rushing in.

There was a lot of commotion, shouting now from them and the last stragglers from the party. I never knew how many people there were that saw, or what story they were given. How it could possibly have been explained.

I was at the front door, my hand on the latch when I heard, 'Grace.'

I turned, looked at my mother.

She saw the case in my hand and then her eyes met mine.

I stared at her, chin out, defiant. I wasn't sorry. Not at all. I knew Jacob was hurt but it was likely he'd live. I was sorry about that, and I knew in that second what I was capable of. I'd do anything for my daughter. Even in vengeance I'd kill for her. I wasn't like Nora McCain and even while worrying thoughts of police and cells pulled at my brain, that one brought some sense of triumph.

She kept my gaze. It was the first time since I'd come home from St Mary's that she'd looked me in the eye.

Just as with Jacob my brain was sparked full of all the things I wanted to say to her.

'I hate you' being the most pressing, but no words came.

Harry was shouting her name; she came to me, and I

wondered if she'd grab me but she didn't. Instead, she reached up around her neck, undoing a chain and pressing it into my hand. Then she turned and went back into the furore, and I stepped out into the cold and empty darkness.

Chapter Eleven

It was closer to morning than midnight by the time I left Fairview Drive, my suitcase in hand, the chain my mother had given me clutched in the other. On it was her wedding ring. The one my father had given her replaced since by one from his own brother. I worked my fingers around and around it as I walked, the cold morning air warming a few degrees as the mists rose. Daylight was starting to break. I walked quickly, purposefully. I knew the way to the train station, and I remembered it was a fair few miles. I expected to be walking an hour and in the end, it turned out to be more.

I passed monotonous fields and familiar places. I'd walked a lot with Daddy, often on Sundays while my mother cooked us lunch. He'd told me that putting one foot in front of the other was as good for the mind as for the body and as I walked that night, I remembered this and I thought he was probably right. By the time I arrived at the train station I felt a peculiar sort of calm. Peculiar because it shouldn't have been there at all.

It occurred to me as I walked towards the little station house why my mother had given me the ring and I slid it off the chain and onto my finger before I walked in. It was light by then and there was a man in the ticket offices looking as bleary-eyed and tired as I felt.

I went up and asked for a ticket to London Victoria. I sat on a small wooden bench, cold now after my long walk. People came into the station in trickles, mainly men in suits who must be commuting to work. Daddy used to do it every Monday morning then home on a Thursday.

I felt an awkward pain at that. An old routine that had been ours for all of my life until the car crash that stole him in seconds, and that wasn't even the worst of my problems.

I wondered what he'd make of me sitting there. Of course, it was a stupid thing to wonder. If he hadn't died, I wouldn't be in this predicament. Someone like Jacob Harse would never have been at our house. There'd have been no St Mary's and no Chloe.

I pressed a hand to my mouth, even thinking her name causing a shudder in me. Dislocation inside.

A voice said, 'Are you OK, miss?'

And I turned and looked at a man, his brow furrowed in concern. I was about to tell him that I was fine and turn away, but I saw a policeman enter the ticket office. My heart started to speed up. I'd been stupid, of course, to think my mother and Harry would just let me go. I'd stabbed one of their guests and stolen from them. I had no idea how much trouble this might put me in, but I figured quite a lot. The train was pulling in, the sound of it chuntering slowly to a halt.

I smiled faintly at the man. 'Do you know, I feel rather fragile, would you mind terribly if I took your arm just while I board the train?'

He stood, offering me his elbow and we walked towards it. The policeman came in, eyes darting to either side, not even stopping on me.

He would be looking for a single girl, not one travelling with a man.

As soon as we boarded the man suggested we might sit together and while I didn't want to be rude, I couldn't bear the thought of making mindless small talk for the hours ahead and I said thank you but no, adding that my husband might not like it. Which seemed to be excuse enough. I held up my hand as if to prove myself.

He said, 'You barely look old enough.'

I smiled, said my goodbyes and walked along until I found an empty carriage. I sat with the red suitcase tucked behind my knees and watched as the landscape changed from rolling fields to red-bricked houses, then finally . . . London.

Chapter Twelve

Mae Scott-Tyler balanced the little boy on one hip, poured hot water on tea leaves and inhaled deeply on her cigarette. It was going to be a warm day and even with the doors open she was bloody boiling. The thing was, Daniel didn't care if it hit a hundred degrees – he'd still want a roast on a Sunday. She opened the oven door, yanking out potatoes, the baby swinging around her body as she went, and grabbing fistfuls of her hair. She shuddered at the thought of what delights might be rubbed into it now but couldn't bring herself to be cross at Sam. He was a lovely little thing. She hadn't wanted him if she was honest and had been livid at Lola for bringing her a child of all things as she pushed towards forty, but now he was here and she wouldn't be without him.

There was a knock at the door. She was the only one in, or the only one awake at least. Lola was upstairs but had yet to show her face despite it being almost midday. Dan and River would turn up for food, probably Byron and the girls would come too. She smiled at the thought of that. She loved having a houseful, loved feeling useful and needed.

She opened the door expecting it to be one of her brood,

but standing on her doorstep was a small girl dressed in fancy clothes with a red leather suitcase and a lost look on her face. 'Can I help you?'

Her eyes were on the baby, not Mae. Mae said again, louder this time, 'Can I help you?'

'Sorry, yes.' Her gaze turned to Mae. 'I hope so. I'm looking for Lola.'

Mae frowned. Girls rarely called for her daughter, more was the shame as far as she was concerned, because boys never stopped knocking, their hopeful faces all grins and smarm until they realised who her father was.

'My Lola?' as if she could mean anyone else.

'I think so.'

The baby wriggled, squirming to get down and Mae levered him with a soft plop, leaning her head back and shouting up the stairs, 'Lola.'

No answer. She sighed, 'She can't always hear me up there.' The only downside to living somewhere bigger than they needed was that she had to holler, often to no avail especially when it came to her daughter, who honest to God slept like the dead. Not that she would ever complain, mind. Mae loved their house. She was proud as anything that her husband, as a young and ambitious man, had managed to earn well enough to take them out of the slums, where they'd both started out. He'd done so well that they'd moved into a property of their own on a nice road and with a good wedge to furnish the place and years more of money coming in. If sometimes she worried about what it was exactly he, and now her son, was up to, she pushed the thoughts away before they took hold.

This time a door slammed and there were feet on the landing. 'Fucking hell, keep your hair on.'

'Language,' Mae hissed, embarrassed in front of this girl, who spoke so nicely.

'Oh my god, Grace. Mum, this is Grace from St Mary's.'

Mae watched her daughter hurry down and hug her friend. Then she pushed her back and looked at her closely. 'What's happened?'

The girl opened her mouth but before she could speak came tears. Mae's heart softened. She could see the girl was in trouble and suspected, rightly, that the next thing would be that she needed a place to stay. 'Come on in, love, I'm doing lunch, we've plenty to go round.'

Daniel Scott-Tyler stared at Mae in disbelief. Another bloody girl in the house. Like the one they already had hadn't caused them enough trouble, which he pointed out to her.

She shrugged. 'Yeah, I know but we wouldn't be without her, would we?' She was smiling, and he felt his resolve weakening. Daniel had a fierce reputation. He was known around London. If there were dodgy, lucrative pies, he had his fingers in them, but he was a sucker, an absolute walkover when it came to his wife. The only thing he'd ever really pushed on was sending Lola away to have Sam. He knew it had broken Mae's heart to be apart from her daughter especially during that time but he'd been adamant. She'd swallowed it as well so he probably owed her one, but it was hard enough getting in the bathroom just with Lola.

He said, 'I mean, Byron and his sisters barely leave at the weekend, do they?' They were, in fact, downstairs now and the noise of conversation and happy laughter wafted up the stairs where Mae and Daniel had retreated for a bit of privacy. Mae had seen the girl's, Grace's, face at the sight of them all; from what Lola had told her the girl had no siblings, so being faced with two sets of loud and fairly rowdy kids was probably quite overwhelming. 'Her mother took her child off her, Dan, gave her away to strangers. Loads of money she has as well, apparently, and the poor girl can't have any more children.'

He screwed up his face, not wanting the details but marvelling at people who wouldn't take in their own. Conveniently forgetting for a moment that in the height of his anger he'd suggested Lola get rid. Luckily, he had Mae to keep him straight. He sighed, 'I mean, that's not right, is it?'

She shook her head. 'Even Gladys never tried to give any of hers away.'

He rubbed a hand across his face. 'See you've been helping the girls sort their place out a bit?'

Mae nodded. 'Yeah, well. Byron's doing well, isn't he?'

'He is. I'm thinking I'll put him up in his own place.'

Mae grinned. Dan added, 'Nothing lavish. But since you can keep an eye on them here.' Her heart swelled. She knew and understood Daniel's reputation. What it had taken for him and Big Des to get where they were was extraordinary. She knew that he had a propensity for violence. Remembered the old days where on a few occasions he'd come home, unable to speak to her or look her in the eye but drenched in blood that wasn't his own. She'd not questioned, not prodded, but had remembered words her mother had flung at her as she'd walked out the door of her childhood home, never to look back. She'd borne it though, had cleaned him in silence, and stood by him no matter what. But she didn't like that side of things. When you came from nothing getting something was always going to be a hard road, but Dan had made his mark, first in the betting kiosks, plying his trade at every race, every match, then the back table of a pub. Now he had his own shop with licence and everything. No, she didn't like how they'd got where they were, but she was grateful to be there. She wondered sometimes if their shared need to take in and care for waifs and strays was an atonement of sorts. Whatever the reason, she wouldn't be turning the little girl away and Dan knew it.

He sighed and lamented as she'd known he would.

Chapter Thirteen

They were people my mother would have hated. People I would once have been scared of but I'd learnt the hard way that soft voices, inherited wealth and education were not precursors for kindness. My own mother's cruelty was indicative of that. Jacob Harse, a grown man, respectable, in the public eye and with a wife, whom I'd been so impressed with on first meeting had ruined my life. There with the Scott-Tylers I found a new kind of life. I healed in their home, in the midst of the ruckus that was their day-to-day lives. Mae fussed in a way my mother never had and I threw myself into being as useful as I possibly could. Which is how I came to take on the role of settler in one of their shops.

It was late on a Thursday night. Lola was asleep, something she did far more than she should, which ought to have alerted us as to her state of mind but didn't. She was adept, I was to discover, at putting on a front and while the Scott-Tylers were definitely a balm after the chilly austere existence I'd had to endure with my mother and Harry, no family were without their problems.

Mae and the baby were sleeping. He was teething by then, little Sam, and prone to waking and causing merry hell in the small hours of the morning. I'd hear him and wake up thinking of my daughter. Her loss was still like a physical pain almost two years later. Via Sam I could chart her, where she would be and what she would be doing. I wondered if she woke in the middle of the night with sore gums and an empty belly. I wondered who went to her, if they loved her even half as much as I did. The kind of thoughts that are bad enough but worsen at three a.m.

It was one of those night where I could hear Mae with the baby that I slipped downstairs meaning to get a drink of water and found River and Byron at the table, pale-faced and surrounded by scraps of paper covered in messy scrawled writing. The first thing I thought as I walked into the kitchen was that I was in my nightclothes, and my face went red. The second was that they looked shifty.

I frowned and River stood, moving fast around me and closing the door behind me. 'If you're coming in, get; I don't want to wake Dad.'

'The baby's up.'

River groaned, slumping forwards, his head in his hands.

I looked to Byron, who met my gaze with steady eyes. I flushed under that look. I was attracted to him, I suppose, even then, but had already relegated anything like that to the back of my mind. Pipe dreams. What man would ever want a woman who couldn't bear him children, and what was the point of marriage without family? Or so I thought then.

I went to the cupboard to get a glass mainly to avoid looking at him, using the time it took to pour a glass of water to compose myself. Even if I was in a nightdress with bare face and naked legs. In the end curiosity won out over my embarrassment and I asked Byron, 'What's going on?'

They exchanged a look and I shrugged, 'OK, don't tell me.'

Then River said, 'Lola said you're clever?'

I sort of shrugged. 'I'm educated.' Which was the truth. Lola had a set of smarts I didn't, as did those young men and Daniel and Mae. I'd realised in St Mary's that, contrary to what I'd always believed, class was born out of capability, hard work and some sort of pre-determined genetic blessing; it was really just the luck of the draw at birth. I knew from Lola how Byron had grown up, had seen the inside of their house, which according to Lola was a step up from where it had been. Dan and Mae were like royalty around London but plenty of their subjects were still stuck in squalor. I saw it every day. Got an education classrooms didn't offer and what amazed me over and over was the sheer resilience it took to live some of their lives.

I knew about Byron's little brother. Almost a year had passed since his disappearance by then, but people still talked about the lad in hushed whispers. I didn't know Byron well but I watched him closely, fascinated by the steely way he had about him, something I recognised in myself. The way certain pains made you harder. I knew his grief must be overwhelming and like me he had no adult to turn to, just younger siblings looking for help.

'So, you're good at numbers, right?'

'Yeah, I'm alright.'

'We're short.'

'What do you mean?'

'The money from the shop, we're short.'

I knew that Daniel owned a pub that had a gym and a small betting shop attached. I went in early to the bar and cleaned the place with Lola by then, though admittedly I did most of the cleaning, keen as I was to earn my keep. I'd offered Mae money from the stash I'd taken from home and she always refused.

I narrowed my eyes at them. 'Short by how much?'

When he told me, my heart leaped into my mouth. River said, 'It's my job. The one bloody thing he trusts me with.' Bitterness edged into his voice, and I felt a wave of pity for him. My eyes met Byron's then and an understanding of sorts seemed to pass between us. I sat down and reached for the scraps, asking, 'These are?'

'All the receipts.'

'Can I get a pen and some paper?'

It took almost four hours. I was shocked by several things; firstly, the sheer amount of money that went through the shop, secondly, that they were clearly attempting to launder a large whack of it and doing it really badly, and thirdly, that without some sort of system they were going to get in trouble.

The money, it turned out, wasn't missing. Everything added up eventually and I could feel the relief between them. I think that was the first time I became aware of the fact that Daniel, who had been kind to me and at home was gentle and placid, was also someone to be feared. The following morning River told him I'd helped with the accounts and would probably be useful in the shop. Which was how I got my first job.

Part II

Now I lay me down to sleep,
I pray the Lord my Soul to keep;
If I should die before I 'wake,
I pray the Lord my Soul to take.

Second rendition, New England Primer (1750)

Every child comes with the message that God is not
yet discouraged of man.

Rabindranath Tagore, Bengali polymath

Chapter Fourteen

Emma woke up and for that second after she opened her eyes she forgot. She forgot that she was living here, in this godforsaken place, in terror, on a knife edge. She'd thought she was so clever, had figured London was the place where all her dreams would come true and, if nothing quite so dramatic happened it might at least be somewhere she would be safe, wouldn't have to fear her mother's latest boyfriend all the time.

For a brief minute it had almost seemed true. She'd taken for granted the room she'd shared with Betty. A hovel was how she'd thought of it. But this place was like a palace, and it was absolute hell. When she met the man, she'd thought this was the answer to all her problems. Betty had given her sharp words of warning and she'd brushed them aside. Laughed and hugged the first real friend she'd ever had and told her not to worry. She'd be back soon. Emma wasn't totally sure how much time had passed but it was a lot. She was either twelve or thirteen, she couldn't quite keep track.

The man had sold her a pup, as Betty put it. Honestly, despite her young age, Emma probably would have given it a swerve in the first place. What had made her change her mind was the woman. She'd spoken to Emma frankly, treated her, she felt, like the adult she'd been forced to be so young. She'd told Emma *you'll live in a beautiful house, wear nice clothes, eat nice food.* She'd nodded, hungry, tired and seduced by what was on offer. Even if she had to do a few things she didn't like, it was well worth it for a roof over her head, food in her belly and a reasonably untroubled day-to-day existence. But, as the days went on, the requests had got worse and worse until she had realised she was no more free here than she had been at home. The house, for all its fancy bedrooms and large walled garden, was a prison and the kindly man and woman who'd rescued her, so she'd thought, from a mean pimp on the streets were even worse. Cold dead devils the pair of them and the company they kept was no better. Visitors to this house were people with soft smiles and voices and hearts like stone.

She was sitting on one of two twin beds with her arm around Benjamin. The poor little bugger was a nervous wreck. She herself was young but she was streetwise and savvy enough; she'd had to be. The boy was hardly nine years old, she reckoned, and he talked all the time about his big brother and sisters whom he missed desperately. He was different from the rest of them in that respect, Benjamin. Of the four children being kept in the house, he was the only one who talked about home. Maybe it was his age, he was the youngest and one of two boys, but she suspected something else too.

He had people who loved him, missed him, ringing not quite alarm bells exactly, but something dimly in her mind knew it didn't add up. Someone had made a mistake.

She knew full well no one was looking for her. There'd be a few other girls, runaways like her forced onto the same shitty street corners who'd notice, and Betty. But she herself had told Betty she was fine, moving on to better things. Those girls would notice when she didn't come back but they wouldn't dwell on it too long. What she didn't have was a mum, dad, aunts, uncles, grandparents or siblings who'd give a shit. Which wasn't to say she didn't have those things. She had two older sisters who'd left home when she'd still been a babe in arms. She couldn't blame them for getting out. It was what she herself had done as soon as she was old enough to work out how to slide a few notes from her mother's purse and make it down to London, but they'd never looked back nor checked on her. Her mum would have been annoyed about the money but, Emma rightly suspected, also pleased to see the back of her third and youngest child. The only advice she'd ever received from the woman was, 'Don't have kids, they ruin everything.' And so far Emma had managed to avoid it. She and the other girl here were given the pill which had come to the fore at the beginning of the decade and was more widely available now as they headed towards the 70s. Nina checked to make sure they took it properly, so she supposed she was safe from that fate at least.

Benjamin was crying in his sleep. She'd come in to check on him and Jackson and was relieved to find they were both there when she arrived back at the domestic side of the house, as Nina so grandly referred to it, in the dark small hours of yet another terrible morning. She ached. Her body burned with pain, inside and out but also something else, something that cut deeper than the nails of the man who'd gripped her arms so hard tonight he'd left crescent-moon imprints from his jagged fingernails.

It was her heart. Her soul that was broken in this nice house, owned by people with smooth voices and even smoother wallets stuffed full of fresh crisp notes. The kind you expected your betters to have. Those voices belied unimaginable horror, rotten, putrid infested minds.

She was coming to the conclusion that there was something very wrong with men. Even the mild punters on the street she couldn't understand. What enjoyment could there be in those shitty transactions formed in car backseats and cold alleys? But they were nothing in comparison to this lot.

Nothing at all. She settled by Benjamin and stroked the little lad's hair back off his forehead. And as he murmured in his sleep, she felt her own eyes filling with tears.

Chapter Fifteen

I was finishing up taking payment from Roy Anselm, who, despite my advice to the contrary, had put down his whole week's wages on the weekend's race. I knew that this meant that his wife, Bridget, a nice woman with a soft face and too many children, would likely show up before payment was due, begging for leniency. He had been granted it last time, but I didn't think he would be again. That meant either Big Des, River or Byron would be sent round. They'd take anything up to the value, which the Anselms were unlikely to have or, more likely, they'd hurt Roy. Which no one wanted. Or which, I perhaps optimistically hoped no one wanted. River and Byron, I would say, weren't naturally violent men, though Byron certainly had more of a stomach for it than River. Lola had told me Byron had seen off a few of Gladys's punters over the years when he'd come of age, and that long before that he'd often be on the receiving end of their fists and boots. I tried to picture the hard, stoic young man who fascinated me with his good looks and cool composure as a frightened young boy and found that actually, it wasn't that difficult.

I myself had changed from something soft and innocent and been battered into the version I was by then. Old me would not have lasted a day in the shop where my time was divvied up between bantering with customers and doing endless sums. I liked both parts equally, but I was well aware that these people would once have scared the crap out of me. Now, I took it all in my stride. Even when there was trouble, which happened from time to time, I didn't panic. I just rang through to the pub and waited in the back office for one of them to come. Frustrated men with little hope spent their cash there along with our more affluent customers. I could see the difference in the two and I encouraged the affluent ones and tried to hand out cautionary tales to the men who, like Roy, were about to blow wage packets they'd never see again. I liked my job. Liked the world I found myself in. People were poor, sometimes scary, often troubled, but they felt more like my people than my own mother did. And I loved Mae and River, Lola and even Daniel, who I was certain wasn't overjoyed with me as a new addition to the family. River liked to play the gangster, the big man. Riding on Daniel's coattails, of course he could, but he had had an easy life in a lot of ways, which made him different from his dad, Big Des and Byron. Byron made me feel different sorts of feelings. Those I was surprised I still had the capacity for. Not that I'd act on them. A young up-and-coming man wouldn't be looking for a barren woman and I instinctively knew that casual relationships wouldn't be for me. I had consigned myself to the single life and that was OK. I was useful to the Scott-Tylers. Useful in the shop. Profit increased quickly, wastage lessened.

The bell rang above the door.

Midday. Byron and River usually showed up at the pub about now for a coffee and something to eat. Byron had taken to leaving River to chat to the regulars and bring me and him lunch while I made coffee. I was never sure, but got the impression that a few of the old boys clung to their old-school racism like a safety blanket and that Byron, while not unwelcome exactly, would never quite fit it. I didn't mind. Not one bit. I looked forward to that hour in the day and the days he didn't make it were never quite as good. That day was no different and we sat in companionable silence, eating sandwiches crammed with doorstep wedges of cheese. Byron looked over the morning's bets and payments. 'Roy's been in again?'

I nodded. 'Silly bugger.'

He shook his head. 'He really is.'

The back door went. Lola wafted in and leant down to give me a quick squeeze. I smiled up at her. 'Coffee's on.'

'Magic.' She poured a cup then pulled a flat quarter bottle of whisky from her pocket and added a generous amount.

Byron frowned at her. 'Aren't you working?'

She grinned at him. 'In a pub.' She tended bar next door and hated it. But on weekends Daniel let her sing and that was the highlight of her week. She had the most beautiful voice I'd ever heard, and the punters all agreed. Despite the fact that she was a pull, Daniel only let her sing if she'd done some shifts of what he called 'grot work' too, which meant tending bar and cleaning up at closing time. I didn't think Byron was keen on her, thought she was a waster; maybe the drinking, which by then was definitely on the increase, reminded him too much of Gladys, who barely pulled a sober breath. Certainly, he had a healthy fear of the stuff and while Daniel, Big Des and River were prone to long binges, Byron always erred on the side of caution.

I could see Lola's faults. She could be lazy, and she was probably spoiled. Daniel let her get away with a lot more than he ever would River, but I also knew that sometimes she'd get a faraway look, and that she snuck out in the middle of the night sometimes to go I didn't know where. I suspected it had something to do with Samuel's dad and I knew well enough to keep my mouth shut, hoping she'd come to me with it eventually.

Lola drank her laced coffee, flicking through a paper she'd brought in with her. Byron and I finished eating and she stood with a sigh. 'I'd better get on with it then.' She put her cup in the sink and I walked her to the back door, giving her a quick hug as she went.

I sat back down at the table looking forward to the half hour Byron and I would have left to chat, and that's when I saw the cover of the now-folded newspaper on the table.

A face staring back at me from the front page that was at once familiar and horrifying. He looked older than I remembered him being and that sent a shudder through me. A man, not even a young man as the dim lights of the garden had made a possibility. He was middle-aged and in a suit. My eyes skimmed the headline. He had been made a member of Parliament. Now he had a cabinet role. He wasn't just anyone 'in politics', he was important. A noise started up in my mind, a faint roar. I was still standing, having been just about to sit. My hands clasped the edge of the table, my fingernails digging into the Formica top. I registered a dull pain in them but knew if I let go too soon, I'd fall. If I fell, I might never get up again.

'Grace?'

Byron's voice sounded very far away. Bile rushed up from my guts, burning through my chest up into my throat. I made it to the toilet just in time, sank onto my jelly wobbly knees, head bowed, whole body shuddering as I retched.

Chapter Sixteen

Big Des was in good form and Daniel found himself laughing so hard his sides hurt. Lola brought them both pints over, and he winked at his daughter who said, 'What's so funny?'

Daniel tapped the side of his nose. 'Never you mind, little one, it's grown-up jokes.'

She rolled her eyes and Big Des grinned at her.

She told them, 'I'm sixteen now.'

That made Daniel laugh all over again and she walked to the other end of the bar, in a huff, he guessed.

Big Des said, 'Hormones, eh?'

Daniel nodded, sombre again now, though he had had a fair few drinks already and was on his way to being quite pissed. 'Yep. She's growing up, I suppose, but she seems so young, you know.'

Big Des said, 'She does a good job here at the weekends.'

Daniel nodded. 'Yeah, sings like an angel. Heart and soul into it. But she's still young and thinks she knows it all.'

'So did we, Dan.'

'Yeah, well, we did, mate, that's the difference. We had to.'

Both men sipped their drinks in silence for a spell.

Daniel's thoughts had turned to the past as he suspected Des's had too. He loved Des as much as he loved any other human. He'd never say it aloud, but they were brothers in heart and spirit if not blood. They'd come up together, both from families that couldn't manage them. Daniel's mother had taken up with a man who used to sneak into his bedroom after dark, an experience that was to mark him for the rest of his life. Only Des knew about it. He'd never even told Mae.

They'd met in a children's home and Dan had recognised Des as a kindred spirit. He was a few years older, too, and took Daniel under his wing. Des had come up with the idea to start running bets and he'd had the size and presence to collect on them. Daniel, it turned out, had a high pain threshold, a violent streak, and good business acumen. They soon made a formidable team. They'd run their first bets, collected the money and committed their first murder together. An old man they'd killed, clinging onto the patch they wanted. Nicholas Salomi, who'd run half of London but lost his sharpness, took his eye off the ball and became a victim of his own arrogance. They'd taken him down when Dan was just fifteen. That had changed him, too. He should probably have felt bad about it but he hadn't. He'd felt powerful. The next person they did in was his stepdad. Daniel had enjoyed that, felt the power slip from the dying man to him. Had known in that second no one would ever take the piss again, and so far, they hadn't. Though there were some unwelcome rumblings being fed back to him and Des, involving Salomi's grandsons, babes in arms back then. Grown men now with a thirst for payback that

73

Dan would not see sated, not ever. That was actually what they'd come to the pub to discuss before getting waylaid.

'Penny for 'em.'

Dan looked at Des, a face as familiar as his own and shrugged. 'Thinking how far we've come.' Des grinned and his reasonably handsome mug was elevated to movie star levels. Women loved them both, that was the truth, and whereas Daniel only had eyes for Mae, Des had never been captured by anyone in particular. And Dan respected it, didn't interrogate his friend though Mae often went on about finding him a nice girl to settle down with.

Des reached out and patted his hand. 'We have. And because we were how we were at sixteen, yours still get to enjoy childhood, eh?'

Dan winced. Des knew, of course, about Lola's pregnancy as he knew everything about them. 'She might think she knows it all, Dan, but she's just a kid and a good one at that.'

Dan smiled. 'You're right.' Des had no children but he was a part of their family. Despite his love for Mae, if she hadn't been able to accept Des as one of them, the marriage would never have happened. Unfair in some ways, especially when you considered she'd had to kiss goodbye to her whole family to marry him, but it's the way it was. Besides, Des would never put him in the position her lot had, where he made him choose.

Des said, 'Don't you worry, Dan. We'll see off these new boys off like we did their idiot granddad.' They'd been visiting a few of their customers, men who took their bets out via Dan and Des, suggesting the Salomis could undercut

74

on repayments which wouldn't do at all. Des said, 'Might be a good time for River and Byron to make their own mark, eh?'

Dan glanced at his son holding court with a few local idiots who hung off his every word. Byron would be the one making the mark, he suspected, though River would likely take the credit. As he was set to take over from Dan it made sense, but Dan did wish his boy was more of a self-starter. People liked River, no one could argue with that. He was charming, good-looking and just so . . . nice. Which was the problem, Dan thought sadly. 'I need a piss.'

He headed off, clapping his son's shoulder as he went and stopping to make small talk with his stupid mates.

Des watched him, mulling over their current irritating situation. They hadn't come this far to be toppled.

'Alright, Des?' He turned to Lola who was all smiles and chest out.

'Not bad, darling.' He flashed her a grin. 'Your dad says you're doing well at the weekends.'

'I'll be famous one day.' There was stubbornness in her voice. Desperate to grow up, she was. Always had been. But like River, she'd been too pampered and cosseted by her parents for the hardship of real life. Des would never say it to his friend, mind, but he felt Dan should have taken a more disciplinarian stance with his children. Feral came out all sorts of ways, after all. He watched her pour a shot of vodka into a coke and knock it back while Dan was out of view; it was that sort of thing he wouldn't have stood for if she was his kid. She grinned at him, and he forced a smile back, keeping his silence. It wasn't his place to lecture her but he also hoped her boozing wasn't going to cause any issues. Dan thought the world of the girl, had been utterly shocked when she'd got her stupid self up the duff.

Despite his and Dan's joking about the new firm, Des felt a touch of real fear over it, as did his friend. They had their own interests to protect. Their own way of doing things. And plenty of endeavours between the two men were on the down low. The last thing they needed was Lola making a spectacle of herself. He'd speak to Dan but carefully.

'No work for you two today then?' She was still smiling, and he could smell the spirit on her breath now. He didn't like women who drank. Dan said she was becoming a woman, and more was the shame, Des thought. She'd been a sweet little girl.

'We're always working, Lo, even when it looks like we're not.'

'Yeah, I know.'

'Speaking of work.' He pointed to a man in the middle of the bar waving a banknote.

'See you soon then, Des.'

He winked, ''Course.'

Chapter Seventeen

Byron was standing waiting outside the door of the toilet. I jumped when I saw him. He was holding out a tea towel from the kitchen. 'Here.'

I dabbed at my forehead which was damp with perspiration, wiped it across my lips and took in a breath that made my shoulders shudder. 'Thanks.'

I held onto it, as he put his hand out. I frowned. 'It needs a wash.'

'Then I'll wash it. Come on, tea.'

I followed him back into the little kitchenette. The paper was gone. I was so relieved my knees wobbled.

He said, 'Sit down, Grace,' in a voice that brooked no argument. I did, partly because I wasn't sure how long I could stay standing.

He made tea not coffee, which we usually had. A man who had perhaps seen his fair share of throwing up and knew that bitterness wouldn't help a disturbed stomach. Any more than sweet tea, which I gratefully received, could help a disturbed mind. I sipped it anyway.

He sat opposite, dark eyes watching my every move and not speaking for what felt like ages. My breathing settled and the judder of fear that had washed through me started to subside.

I put the cup down. He said, 'What did he do to you?'

I shook my head and he reached across the table, took my hand in his. 'My mother, God bless her soul, is a useless woman. You know that.'

I nodded, super aware of his fingers intertwined with mine. I looked at them resting there and marvelled at how natural it felt. How little I was scared as I had always considered I might be if in close contact with a man. Byron was big. Six foot plus, broad and strong. Bigger than Harse. He could hurt me just as bad, if not worse, but I didn't believe for a second that he would. I realised then that I trusted him and with that came the first glimmers of something approaching hope. Maybe I wasn't quite so shattered as I thought. Maybe something resembling normality wasn't so far out of reach that there was no point trying.

'She should never have had kids and yet there she was with four of us before she was barely grown herself. Her job was a dangerous thing, but she doesn't have to do it anymore and I say that with no small amount of pride because that's down to me. Dan gave me the opportunity and I'll always be grateful; no one else would employ me because of the colour of my skin.' He grinned then, and I thought it was the saddest smile I'd ever seen. 'But I am the one that shows up. I do the work. Things I'd prefer not to if I'm honest but I do it because it puts food in the mouths of my siblings. Makes the hellhole we were dragged up in bearable. But it can't bring back my brother and it can't take away my memories. When I was a child, I lived in constant fear. It's hard to explain it exactly but I hardly slept, and all of the awful, terrible things I could imagine were going to happen; to me, to my mum, to my sisters and little brother, came along with plenty worse, too. The most awful thing of all, of course, was Benjamin going. You never met him, but I wish you had. He was sweet in a way I'm not, the girls aren't and I never remember Mum being. A natural sunny disposition, even born into the chaos that was us. Whenever things were shit, I'd go and play with him, read a story. No matter how dark the world, his light gave me some measure of comfort, of faith. Now he's gone. My heart is broken in a permanent way. A way it won't ever heal from. I see the same marks in you. The same pain and I'm warning you that poison will sit inside of you and fester, Grace, if you don't find some way to deal with it, and letting it out can help.'

A silence. Tears I hadn't even known I was crying slipped down my cheeks, catching on my lips, salt on the end of my tongue. Poison in my soul. His hand released mine, reached up to my face, wiped a hard calloused thumb across my cheek. I was surprised to find a fizz of desire at that action.

'When I find out who took Benjamin, I will kill them. Even if he is alive and well, which I admit I hope for more than is wise.' A pause. I cry my silent tears. He is my witness. 'Who is that man, Grace, and what did he do to you?'

I didn't say anything and then I took a deep breath and I spoke. For how long I didn't know. To start with my voice was barely a whisper and I heard my own words, saw my own story as it was. I told Byron I didn't want to be a victim for the rest of my life, that I refused that role, but that

I also knew I was changed. That as he missed Benjamin, I was lost without Chloe; a piece of me had been snatched from my arms and given to strangers.

The words spilled, halting and stilted and then fast like I couldn't stop saying it all if I tried. The last time I'd spoken the truth it had been to my mother, for all the good it did me, and even Lola didn't know about the stabbing.

I paused when I got to that part and looked up to meet his eyes. He was unwavering, letting me speak, his face not belying the horror I felt, at my own actions and my complete lack of remorse for them.

I was finished and there was a silence. Deep and heavy as if sacred sound had snuck into its fibre. I felt . . . lighter. I felt almost free.

'Byron.' It was River, head poking round the door from the pub, taking in our held hands. Byron didn't move away.

'Coming, man.'

He walked around the table and knelt before me, tucking my hair back behind my ear. Then he leaned into me, pressing his lips so gently on mine it almost tickled. Then he was gone, taking my story and the newspaper with him.

Chapter Eighteen

It was late by the time Lola and Grace got in. Mae was like an unsettled hen. She was well used to Daniel and River keeping late hours, but she was less comfortable with it being the girls. Especially Grace who despite blending in with the family, and the wider community so well, wasn't streetwise like the others were. Daniel was insistent, though, that Lola pull a few shifts at the pub. He was concerned, he said, that she'd either end up bone idle or pushing out too many kids too fast. Mae had her own fears about her daughter, but hadn't voiced them to Daniel who was a worrier anyway when it came to the kids.

She heard the key go and had to restrain herself from jumping up and heading to the door. Lola would only roll her eyes at her mother. Whispering from the hallway and banging now. Lola laughed and Grace shushed her. She was a good girl, Grace, but also not to be underestimated. Mae could see that in her. She had steeliness and she was smart. Book smart as well as the other kind. River said she'd revolutionised the shop, which was pulling in almost obscene amounts of money. Plus, she'd come up with all kinds of ideas for linking punters from the shop to the pub and vice versa. 'Integrating,' she called it. Business acumen.

Something Mae herself possessed. Daniel and Big Des had been feral lunatics when she'd met them. Making cash but only by menaces. She'd finessed their techniques. Moved them up in the world.

To say Dan had been rough round the edges when they met was an understatement. She liked to think she'd helped soften and refine him. Certainly, the pub and the shop had been her idea. Setting them up had been fine but they hadn't held her interest once the kids were there, so it was nice to see Grace stepping in, though a voice at the back of her mind said, 'Be wary.' Not that she'd say it aloud and not that she expected Grace to try to usurp her or the family but you never knew. A girl unable to have a family of her own, after all.

That's why she always thought of Sam so much, Mae supposed. Her heart went out to the girl. She'd have been a good mother and from what she'd garnered from Lola, she'd asked her mother to let her keep the bairn and the woman had said no. Mae couldn't imagine it. There'd been talk by Daniel of not keeping Lola's babe and Mae had listened with only half an ear. She'd never turn away blood. No matter what. Her family was her life. Sam was indeed fast asleep, but that baby would sleep happily through World War Three without so much as a peep and she headed out into the hallway to remind the girls of this truth.

What greeted her was Grace desperately trying to get Lola's shoes off and Lola, falling down drunk.

'What the hell?'

'Mummy,' followed by a peal of cackling.

Mae pressed her lips into a thin line and Grace said, 'Sorry. I was trying to get her to bed.'

Mae shook her head. 'Hardly your fault, is it?' It came out sharper than she meant, and she saw Grace wince.

She sighed, patting the girl's arm which was stick thin. 'Get her in here and let's try to get her sorted before her father comes in.'

They managed to corral Lola into the living room where they plonked her unceremoniously onto the sofa and she promptly passed out. Grace's face was ashen, and she leaned in to her friend. 'Is she alright, do you think?'

'Not used to drunk people?'

Grace shrugged. 'My mum and dad didn't like it.' Adding by way of explanation, 'She started to drink once Uncle Harry moved in, mind. I avoided it then, don't love it now. The loudness.'

Mae nodded. She understood alright. Her Daniel liked a drink, always had, and him and Big Des could tear one on. Were often gone for days. Less so at that point but when they'd been young she found it hard. The thing was, Mae had believed in Daniel. He'd given her an impassioned speech about wanting more than he was supposed to expect. More than society said a boy like him should have. She understood it. Poverty. Had been part of a happy enough family but they were surrounded by others less fortunate, not that they had a lot, mind. Nothing like Mae's kids had. And she'd seen kids dragged up hard as hell in the same streets, without a pot to piss in. A lot of the old-timers around them were prone to romanticising it: 'Well, we had nothing and still thrived.' Another favourite was

83

the 'strong sense of community', which they claimed had existed then, especially during the war. Mae and Daniel had just been kids then really, but he saw it how she did. A shithole, full of desperate, angry adults wondering where their next meal was coming from and too many kids for anyone to clothe and feed.

Dan had it far worse than her, of course, no denying he and Big Des experienced a terrible time. In and out of care homes and other charitable institutions where, Mae suspected, they were badly abused, as children in those situations sometimes are.

Mae's family weren't wealthy but they had had enough, and her parents had been kind, loving people. Just thinking about them made her feel weepy. Her mother was still alive and not far away either, and her brother, of course. What he was up to now, she didn't know. Didn't want to know. She was sure her mother, Sophia, still looked after him if he needed it. This is what she told herself. They had each other at least.

Never mind all that now, Mae thought, as she looked at her own daughter, a wave of shame spreading over her. Like her own mother before, who'd had a deep bond with her brother that the two females hadn't really shared in the same way, she, if not exactly favoured, definitely found River easier in comparison to Lola.

She looked at her beautiful, incredibly young daughter now, absolutely sparko on the expensive sofa and thought, for all their money and stability, it hadn't saved the girl from pain. And pain was what Lola was in. Any idiot could see that.

Mae glanced at the clock, aware that Dan would probably be in soon and wondering if she was going to manage getting Lola upstairs. As if reading her mind Grace said, 'Shall we get her into bed?'

Mae nodded, grateful. 'You take her legs, OK?'

They managed it with only a few stumbles. Grace helped Mae undress her friend, putting her in a nightdress with Mae sighing, 'I hate the thought of her not brushing her teeth.'

Grace smiled. 'We'll make sure she does it twice in the morning, eh?' And then, 'Sam slept through it.'

'Nothing wakes him other than hunger.' Mae said.

Grace nodded but it was a sad gesture. Looking at her properly, Mae thought she herself looked like she'd been crying and thought about asking her, but Grace said, 'I think she'd been drinking for most of her shift. Vodka.'

Mae shook her head. 'How long?'

'What?' A deer caught in headlights. Teenagers, all of a kind, would sweep in to protect their friends.

'How long has she been like this, love?'

Grace shrugged, studied her feet as though they were the most interesting thing she'd ever seen.

'Come on, Grace, I'm not an idiot. I've smelt it on her. Seen her taking nips from our bottles. Only Dan ever goes into them, so I notice.'

Grace sighed. 'I don't know.'

'It'll be over a boy, I suspect.'

Grace nodded. 'Sam's dad, I'd say.'

Mae's ears pricked up at that. 'You know who that is?'

Grace shook her head, told Mae, 'No.' And Mae believed her.

Her daughter, who usually couldn't keep anything to herself, even when the situation required it, had sat on this secret for almost two years. Mae had a few of her own, of course: secrets, you didn't get to her age without them; but she was sad that Lola had chosen deceit and subterfuge already. Because that's what this was. Withholding the truth from her family who loved her. She could understand her not telling Daniel. She herself would have been tempted to keep it from him if she knew. His temper, though more in check these days, could flare up and when it did it was as ugly as it had ever been.

It wasn't normally aimed at them though and she herself had felt real fear when he'd found out Lola was in the family way.

She said to Grace, 'I didn't blame her. For keeping it to herself.'

Grace nodded. 'Daniel would have laid into him?'

Mae smiled at the girl's well-articulated voice wrapping itself around their own rough language. 'He would, yes, or worse still forced Lola to marry him, which I thought would be terrible for her.' She shrugged. 'Dan and I were her age when we met, did you know that?'

'I guessed you were young.'

Mae nodded. 'Babes really, but he'd had a hard time, I was ready to go out into the world, we found refuge with each other. But we weren't like Lola, we'd grown up fast because we had to.' Mae paused, trying not to remain on that thought. She'd had to grow up fast because she'd left her family home, of her own accord though she had felt at the time she had no choice. 'When she told me she was pregnant . . . God.' She pressed a hand to her mouth, recalling the horror. The icy fear that had spread through her. 'She was a child. She still is.' She looked at her daughter, who appeared younger still at rest. It still made her uncomfortable, the pregnancy, and she had a mother just a few years older than Lo was now.

She said to Grace, 'Should I have let her keep Sam, as hers, I mean?' suddenly and unusually desperate for some reassurance, and she found that this young girl with the old soul's opinion mattered right now.

Grace shook her head. 'No. I don't think Lola could look after him. You're right, she was too young – still is. And that's not what's eating her. Like you said, it's the bloke.'

'And you've no idea . . .'

'No. None.' She was looking away now, unable to meet Mae's eye.

Mae took a deep breath, reaching for her hand and squeezing it. 'Grace. My daughter is in trouble. I want to help her. If there's something you know . . .'

Grace sighed and ran a hand over her face. 'Can I make a cup of tea? I'm so tired.'

They went downstairs. Mae made the tea, though Grace offered. She hated other people doing things in her kitchen. Besides, she needed the girl to talk.

She sat opposite and looked at her levelly. 'Come on, Grace.'

'She's my best friend. My only friend.'

Mae said, 'We all have your back now, Grace.'

And Grace nodded at the truth of the words, her mind spreading also to the intense lunch she'd shared with Byron. The welcome the Scott-Tylers had given her as soon as she'd turned up unexpectedly on their doorstep. She fit here in this mad world she hadn't been bred for. Mae was a good mother, brilliant. For all Nora McCain's airs and graces she'd failed fundamentally at parenting and to Grace, who knew she'd never bear children she'd get to hold and raise and love, it was anathema.

All that aside, she, too, was worried about Lola. She could see where she was headed, and it was nowhere good.

'When I first got here, she was OK, wasn't she?'

Mae thought about it. 'I suppose she was, yes.' She recalled her daughter arriving home. There had been a few months where the girl readjusted, recovered physically because birthing was one discombobulating bitch no matter how tough you thought you were.

'She used to sneak out.'

Mae froze. Her first thought was that Dan must never find out. She took a sip of her tea, enough time to make her voice come out steady because she was annoyed now as well as cornered. They had rules here. Boundaries. She showed her love for her children with affection, yes, but there was an expectation that they reciprocated in kind. Their job was to toe the line. Her children hadn't given her much trouble. She worried about them, of course. Always would. She worried that River was stuck in his father's shadow. That while she knew Dan loved the boy, he perhaps didn't respect him. She worried that Lola was directionless and lazy. Floating through life, dreamlike, looking for the easiest way. She defended both of them to Dan, of course, and understood why her husband had made a deal with Lola regarding her singing in the pub. She did need to learn the value of hard work. At little older than her, she and Dan had embarked on setting up the lucrative businesses they ran now. Neither of Mae's children would have the gumption to do what they had. But surely that meant they'd done their job right? You always wanted better for your kids, didn't you? For them to have an easier, softer ride of it.

She sighed. 'When?'

Grace shrugged. 'Early hours of the morning.'

'You talked about it?'

Grace nodded. 'I asked her. She wouldn't tell me details but I was concerned. Wandering about at that time.'

Mae nodded agreement. Grace said, 'Her bloke picked her up, at the end of the road.'

'In a car?'

'Yes, dropped her back a few hours later.'

This made Mae's heart sink. A boy older than her if he was driving, and that timeframe could really only mean one thing. He was using her for sex. Mae tried to push the thought away, but it sprang back – what other reason could there be?

Then the obvious one occurred to her: it was someone she knew her family would disapprove of.

'How was she, those nights when she got back?'

'Honestly? Floating on air.'

She and Grace finished their tea and when the girl went up Mae poured herself a small glass of whisky and sat at the kitchen table, smoking and making a mental list of her husband's enemies. It turned out they were legion. You didn't get where the Scott-Tylers were without ruffling feathers along the way. She liked to think that her husband kept within the reasonable rules laid out in the underworld, but he'd taken out the man who came before him to earn his seat and his kids — girls, so not a big threat — had grown children now. Their enemy's grandkids and they were sniffing around. The Salomi's. It'd be one of them. First thing in the morning she'd start her own investigation. No matter what, she'd get to the bottom of this and she'd help her daughter.

Chapter Nineteen

Daniel was drunk, sure, but his brain still didn't miss a trick. More was the pity for River who sat at the bar, head hung low, while his father lambasted him for his perceived failings. There'd been a mix up with some money owed and what was collected. River had settled a debt for lower than it should have been. He'd missed a zero, so it was a simple mistake but a humiliating one.

Byron understood it to some degree. It put Dan and Big Des in a tricky situation for sure. If they went round now, begging for the remainder, or even kicking some serious arse for the remainder which was more likely, it wouldn't look good at all. Not least because Dan liked his reputation as benevolent hardman. Scary as fuck, but fair with it. It was also liable to fall on Byron's shoulders, a thought he didn't relish as he could hardly blame the man for paying less when he was told that was what he owed. They'd look a bit shitty.

The guy who owed the cash had obviously felt all his lucky days had come at once and no one could expect the ponce to say, oh, actually I owe you a ton more. The guy would likely be looking over his shoulder and really, he should have said something, of course he should.

But it didn't change the fact it was their . . . well, River's mistake.

Dan was so enraged spit flew from his mouth as he bellowed at his son. Byron could see River clenched and struggling to keep control. The main trouble was, Dan expected too much of River. He expected him to be just like him, but the truth was River wasn't as savvy and he wasn't as hard either. He was nicer than Daniel, by far. Byron didn't fall for Dan's good guy act, though he appreciated that he excelled at family life. Envied River that to a large degree. But River could never be Dan. He hadn't had the struggle it took to sharpen your edges and toughen up your heart. He was a charmer, an excellent salesman and that's where his talent should be utilised in Byron's opinion. Not that anyone asked for it and he wasn't stupid enough to give it unsolicited either. Though he was considering weighing in on this.

Big Des sat watching the whole thing through steady eyes. Byron studiously avoided looking at the big, handsome man who honestly gave him the creeps though he couldn't say exactly why.

He never gave out to anyone really, but Byron reckoned he gave Dan the go-ahead on everything, that he had the final say. Even when it came to his own kids.

'What do you have to say? Eh?'

River flinched. 'What do you want me to say?'

'Fuck all. That's the problem, I just want . . .'

'What, Dad?' The boy met his eyes now and they stood glaring at each other. 'What? Want me to be better at maths?'

'Fucking competent would do.'

'It was an honest mistake, human error.'

'And now I look like a mug.'

Byron had had enough. He coughed, and three sets of eyes turned back to him. 'Pat does a few runs for the Salomis, right?'

Dan glared at him. 'Which makes this sting all the more.'

'But maybe we could use that, and this, to our advantage.'

Dan was still looking at him like he was mad, but Byron had started so he'd have to finish. 'Like maybe we go see him, point out the mistake, which absolutely benefits him, of course, and remind him he's lucky we're not taking him out over it.'

'Let the money go?' Dan's voice was high, incredulous. Byron forced himself to stay steady, calm eyes meeting Dan's.

'Hear the boy out.' Big Des, quiet but not stupid. Giving the go-ahead again. He was in charge, thought Byron. They were partners to all intents and purposes, but Big Des had a calm control that Dan lacked, and Dan turned to him for things.

Dan settled back down on his bar stool and snapped at River, 'Make yourself useful and pour us all a drink then, eh?'

Byron carefully avoided looking at the boy he'd come to consider a good friend. His humiliation was complete. You could feel it in the air, and Byron witnessed it in River's slouch out of the corner of his eye, as he went to do Dan's bidding. Mae, he thought to himself, never sees this stuff.

The only thing he could think to help River was this, even if it annoyed him even more.

'You speak,' Dan commanded as River set three tumblers out for them all. Byron glanced at his but didn't touch it. Hated the stuff with a passion but knew better than to say so.

'We go see Pat, tell him it was our mistake but the fact is he still owes us a load.'

Dan exhaled like a bull about to impale a matador. Des put a hand on his shoulder and said to Byron, 'Then?'

'Then we say, being benevolent and generous we're willing to let it go if he does us a small favour.'

'Spying on the Salomis?' Big Des grinned.

Byron nodded.

Dan muttered something incoherent.

Big Des said, 'I like it. Those little fuckers are popping up in all kinds of sly ways. The daughters from that family were as useless as charred wood but the grandsons . . .' He shook his head. He was referring to Timmy and Mason and, Byron thought, Des and Dan had good reason to be concerned. They were sharp young men and disgruntled. Their mums had been a soft lot and married soft useless men, too. Kids spouted out at the peak of Nick Salomi's empire and wealth. Dan and Des had taken the lot and whistled cheerfully while they did it. In one generation they lost if not everything, then most of it. Timmy and Mason were angry, clever and driven.

If Byron was honest, he'd have approached them for work eventually, but where he had landed was the way the cards had been dealt and Dan and Des's enemies were now his by inheritance.

Dan was nodding now. 'Yeah. Good plan.' He slapped Byron's shoulder. 'Well done, lad.' And glared at his son. 'At least someone round here is using a few brain cells.'

Dan and Des dismissed the two younger men, and Byron and River headed out. It had been a warm summer, pleasant and not too humid but at three in the morning it was still cold and Byron felt a shiver as they went into it.

They walked in silence for a few minutes. Byron could almost hear his friend trying to put things into words. His anger, Byron suspected, was about to come out sideways.

And he was right. 'Have fun sucking up to my old man?'

'Not much and I wasn't sucking up, I was saving you from having to annihilate Pat.'

'Oh, so you think I'm thick as shit, too?'

'No.'

River had stopped now, and Byron met his gaze. Let him huff and puff, which he did. He was shorter than Byron, not by much but enough that the intimidation was almost farcical. Byron didn't laugh, though. Had no desire to. River was his friend. Eventually River seemed to almost collapse, shoulders slumping, head down and they started walking again. 'He's never liked me.'

Byron said, 'He's your dad, he loves you.'

River nodded, kicked a stone that skittered across the pavement and down a drain, making a tinkling sound as it went. 'I know he loves me. Mum wouldn't have it any other way, but he doesn't like me.'

Byron kept his peace. There was truth in those words and he was not in the business of stealing that from people. People had a right to their own stories even when they hurt. He'd seen that in Grace as she spoke. Hadn't interrupted her, hadn't broken her flow and hadn't said, 'There, there.' Sometimes life was a cunt and that needed acknowledging, witnessing, not turning a blind eye to.

'I hardly ever make mistakes, but when I do it's always with numbers.' He shook his head. Byron knew this. Had seen River struggle a few times. 'I'm not dumb, though.'

'I know.'

'I'm not being used for the right things.'

'Yeah, I know that too.'

'What should I do?'

Byron shrugged. 'Right now? Fuck all. We play the game.'

'We?'

'Not being presumptuous.' Byron held his hands up but River grinned. 'I didn't want to work with you, you know.'

Byron shrugged.

'I mean, not because of . . .' he waved a hand. 'I don't care about colour or any of that. The old boys are way too concerned with that sort of shit and half of them originate somewhere else.'

Byron said, 'Tribal, isn't it, some innate thing.'

'Whatever, that isn't it for me.'

'What was it then?'

'Your mum, your family. My dad's a fan of "we all make our own luck." Before I met you, I figured that was the truth of it. Like I was ahead because I had more sense, worked harder.'

'Right.' Byron's jaw was clenched now. He resented what River was saying.

'That's not the case though, is it? I'm where I am 'cause of who my dad is. You were where you were because of your mum.'

'Probably.'

'My mum said she could have been Gladys if the cards were dealt different.'

Byron snorted. He liked Mae, had a lot of respect for her. 'I doubt it.'

'We'll never know, will we? But I recognise I've had more luck than you in a lot of ways.'

Byron appreciated that and he patted River's shoulder; it was this side of his son that Daniel didn't fully appreciate. The genuine good-heartedness of River. Byron said, 'The way your dad is towards you is tough, man, ain't saying it's not.'

'But it's what I've got right now, eh?'

'It is. But it won't be forever.'

River laughed, a bitter, brittle sound. 'Fucker'll probably outlive us all.'

Byron laughed along with this boy he used to envy so much and who now, just in this second, envied him. A young man who had become his best friend.

But he felt uneasy still and was not quite sure why.

Chapter Twenty

I woke early the next morning to the sounds of Lola groaning. I got a cold glass of water and a damp flannel, then returned to her. She looked deathly. Her beautiful colouring, fiery red hair, pale skin, dark eyes were all somehow dulled. I dabbed her forehead and helped her sit. As I fed her sips of water, she said, 'My dad?'

I shook my head. 'He was in the bar early evening. Came back after River came and told me to get you.'

She nodded. Relieved, I supposed. I realised she didn't remember much about the night before and marvelled, not for the first time, at the draw of something so harmful, so lethal it could wipe your memory. Yet people still longed for it, still imbibed. I supposed that was why and maybe I did get it a bit. But as much as I had things I longed to forget, I needed to be in control more. Losing that would terrify me.

I said, 'Mae was awake when we got in though.'

Lola slumped back onto the bed, a hand pressed across her face. 'Shit.'

'We, well, she thinks the pub isn't the best place for you.'

Lola frowned. 'I like singing.'

Grace shrugged. 'I don't know about the singing, you'll have to talk to her, but you're coming to work with me.'

'In the shop?'

I nodded.

'What the fuck?'

'It's not bad.'

'Looks bloody boring to me.'

I sighed at that. 'But you might get from one end of the day to the other sober there.'

She sort of flinched. 'God, I can't remember anything.' She pulled her long legs up, resting her head on them. She looked impossibly young and terribly fragile.

I said, 'It was fine really. The worst part was the walk home and that was just you and me.'

'Oh, mate. I'm sorry.'

I smiled, going for nonchalant, though trying to carry someone bigger than me most of the walk back hadn't been ideal. Worse than trying to get her to physically get going had been the tears. Over and over she'd told me, 'He said he loved me.' And every time I'd asked who, she'd clammed up. Even in that state she'd kept it in, held it to herself. After she went to bed, passed out, Mae and I had had our chat. I was uneasy about it. I'd betrayed Lola's confidence to some degree whichever way I looked at it and I was sorry for that. But I was worried about her, too. Really worried. When I'd got to the pub, River was livid. Said she'd been about to walk off with some random bloke. That was a new and dangerous addition. Most blokes would leave Lola well alone. She was, after all, the young daughter of a known face but not all had the common sense to stay away. Since she'd already been in trouble once I knew the last thing Mae wanted was a repeat. Their family had a capacity for love that my mother didn't. I watched them all with Sam. I watched them with each other. They were easy, affectionate. How, I guessed, things should be. How my dad was with me. I blinked away tears at his memory and forced a smile on my face for Lola. 'Come on, it'll be fun. Some of my customers will have you in stitches.'

Lola smiled back but it was a far cry from the cheeky grin I'd found so enchanting at St. Mary's. The bloke had ended it. That's what I thought. Lola had expected to come home, hand the baby over and get back to it with him and he'd had other plans. Just twenty-four hours ago I wouldn't have even been able to imagine a broken heart but after Byron's kiss . . . My feelings for him, I realised in that moment, made me vulnerable. I pushed the thought away. I didn't need to deal with it then and there. 'Come on, Lo. Get up, get dressed, eh?'

Mae wanted me to keep an eye on her. That's why we were being put where we were.

She was a good mother, Mae. Fiercely protective and also a natural problem-solver. The thing was, I wasn't as certain as her that Lola could be fixed quite so easily, and it would turn out that I was right.

The day wasn't too bad. Lola, despite her act to the contrary, wasn't stupid or incapable and I watched her take bets, chat to customers, her natural charm shining through, and by lunchtime I'd say she was relaxed and almost enjoying herself. Byron nipped in as usual and I was grateful Lo was there, that it meant I didn't have to deal in any way with what had passed between us the day before. I felt a thrill at his presence, though, despite myself and as he was leaving, he squeezed my shoulder. Two seconds after he left Lola said, 'You gonna tell me then?'

I frowned as I turned the closed sign to open, her trailing behind me. 'Tell you what?'

We both settled behind the cash desk. I was looking straight ahead but could feel her eyes on me like they were burning into my mind. 'What's going on with him?' Her head jerked towards the kitchen which Byron had just vacated.

I laughed and it sounded nervous and forced. 'We have lunch. You know what they are like in the pub. He and River go in there to eat, no point buying out. River stays there, Byron's started nipping in here, that's all, no big deal.'

'Oh, yeah?'

I nodded, heat rising in my face, which I was sure was the colour of beetroot. Luckily for me, I was saved from having to answer by the bell of the door and a customer.

Chapter Twenty-One

The house was too full, and Emma felt wobbly. She understood that Nina slipped things into the younger children's drinks. With Emma, she just gave her the pills now. When Emma had lived with Betty, Betty had warned her about the perils of drugs. Her view was you did the work for as short a time as you could and ultimately tried to meet a nice bloke and use marriage as a way to get off the streets. If you were out of your head ninety percent of the time, that brought with it a whole new host of problems, ones that might kill you and at the very least would ruin your life. No doubt.

Now Emma didn't even think before she swallowed what Nina gave her. Betty would be horrified and even that thought made oblivion look oh so sweet. Whatever she had taken the night before had wiped clean away almost a whole twenty-four hours. Unfortunately for Emma, though, the missing time always came back eventually. Drip feeding from her dreams, bleeding into daytime. Awful, unthinkable things that explained the miscellaneous pains she found in various parts of her body. The men who visited this place were animals, a small select group of humanity's most awful humans, but Nina was somehow worse. Emma had liked her, a lot. She'd come back after the big man had spoken to her a few times. He'd been kind, polite, respectful even. Nina had approached her and introduced herself as a concerned friend of his. It had been after a particularly terrible time in a car with a man who wasn't satisfied with Emma's services. He'd shouted, which had scared her. She found it almost laughable that that had been among the worst things that had happened to her. Things here proved to her that no matter how bad it got, there was always another layer of fuckery to be had.

Benjamin and Jackson were quiet as mice. She noted Benjamin's wide, blue eyes were glassy. She forced herself to look away. The only thing more terrible than what befell her on a day-to-day basis was the knowledge that sooner rather than later a similar fate would be his and Jackson's. Babies they were and already one man, whom she thought Ben already knew, was there, buttering them up with gifts and cuddles. Babies, for Christ's sake. These sick people had no respect for that fact, no conscience. She'd seen Nina cuddling Ben and seen Ben wrap his arms around her. It had made her feel sick. But she herself had been just the same and she was older, far more worn down than the little boys were.

The blond man with the floppy hair and a smile like the Cheshire cat from *Alice in Wonderland* plonked down next to her, arm sliding across her thin shoulders. She remembered loving that book. They'd read it at school and Emma had imagined herself slipping into a different reality and having adventures of her own. As she travelled from her hometown to this godforsaken city, which landed her in this beautiful prison, she'd still entertained fantasies of all the things she might do. The ways she'd be free, far from her abusive parents. Her adventures had turned out to be more of a horror story though.

The man slid a hand up her bare thigh and she forced herself to grin at him because she'd learnt it was usually easier that way.

She felt fragile next to him. Next to all of them, as though they might just break her at any second and she'd be powerless to stop it, which she would, and which they might.

Grogginess pervaded her mind. She was aware of the man taking her hand, yanking her up from the sofa and him keeping up a constant stream of chatter which she couldn't keep up with. And then everything drifted to nothing and it was the following morning. Her body was sore and she'd undressed. Next to her she heard Ben whimpering. She wrapped her arms round him, pulled the little boy close and told him, 'It'll be OK.' Hating herself for the lie but having nothing else to offer him of any use.

Chapter Twenty-Two

Byron had laid everything out, slowly and calmly to Pat.

Pat was twitchy and looked fast from Byron to River then back again. 'He told me the wrong amount.'

'You didn't correct him though, did you?'

Pat laughed but it sounded more insane than comical. ''Course I fucking didn't. My old gal will have me guts for garters if she found out I'd spunked my whole wage packet.'

Byron leaned back in his chair. Pat's concern was a shitty little newsagent's that sold out-of-date crap. Byron knew the Salomis used it to launder cash, hence their connection to this idiot, and also that Pat was the kind of man who would always spend more than he had before he had it and thus be at the mercy of men like him and River. And the Salomis.

'You more scared of her than us, eh, Pat?'

'You fucking seen her?' He tried for a smile, but it fell off his face before it got started. Byron could see the beads of perspiration building on his forehead. He was scared. Trying not to show it but Byron and River's reputation preceded them. Byron had done things that woke him in the middle of the night. Things he would never have done if he'd had any choice. Things he knew left an indelible stain on his soul. His reputation was that of a lunatic, which was exactly what Dan and Des wanted to portray. He played along with it and doing those things once hopefully meant he wouldn't need to do them again.

Pat knew. Had heard the rumours, bad enough in their naked truth, utterly unpalatable by the time they became exaggerated on the street. He was looking at the two young men in front of him with horror, as well he might. Byron met his gaze with a sinister smile. He didn't want to hurt Pat. He needed him to agree, not least because it would mean he had Des's ear, which he would need if he wanted to rise up, as he did. Now he'd had a taste of the difference money could make, not just for him, not even mainly for him, but for his siblings and his mum, who no longer had to sell her arse on shady street corners. Money also gave him status and that was something he craved. Having been shat upon and spat upon his whole life for a variety of misdemeanours, most of which weren't even in his control, Byron wanted power. Needed it in a world that seemed set to keep it just out of reach.

Pat sank in on himself. 'I ain't got it.'

Byron held his hands out in front of him, almost jovial now. One pal chatting to another. 'And like you said, Pat, it was our mistake and not yours.'

Pat nodded, mumbled, 'That's right.' But the sweat was still coming, snaking down his ruddy cheeks.

Byron nodded along. Pat could tell there was a trap of some kind, a sting coming his way but he couldn't see what. Men like him were useless lumps as far as Byron could tell. He had inherited this place, a little shop with flat above. Given everything on a plate and still managed to run himself, his wife, and his kids into poverty. Still managed to end up the plaything of two wannabe London gangsters. Actually, Byron felt fairly certain at some point the Salomis would triumph. They'd take over what Dan and Des had one day and he himself knew he'd be flexible on who his employer was, too. Loyalty was fine but he was disposable to Dan and Des, he knew that. River was another matter. Byron considered him brethren now, and he suspected River felt the same way towards him. Whatever, these were concerns for a future date.

He leaned across, so his face was close to Pat's. 'You do a little bit of business with the Salomi boys.'

At that very moment Byron witnessed the man cave. The corners of his mouth turned down, shoulders slumped. 'I don't know what you mean.'

Byron laughed, River did, too. The two playing off each other.

There was a silence then. Fine for Byron who was always comfortable when no one spoke. Fine for River who would be the one to break it. Excruciating for Pat who honestly wondered if he was about to have a heart attack.

Byron settled back. River moved closer. It had been three minutes, which didn't sound like long but felt like forever when it was used to let fear fester. 'You alright, Pat?'

River's voice was barely a whisper, but Pat jumped as they'd known he would. 'We need you to be our eyes and ears, Pat.' Pat didn't answer, just sat trembling as another painful silence engulfed him.

Byron said, 'Now, let's cut the crap because I don't want to have to use my bag of tricks.' He kicked the duffel at his feet which made an ominous rattling sound and elicited an actual whimper from Pat.

Byron grinned. 'I don't want to ruin me new suit. Nice, isn't it?'

Pat looked at him like he was mad, which was exactly the impression Byron aimed to give him. Like he was a loosely coiled spring capable of great and life-changing violence, which in fairness, he was. When he had to commit such acts, he used lots of things for fuel. His father whom he'd never met, his mum's punters and boyfriends, especially the ones who'd battered and attacked him and his siblings over the years. Everyone who'd called him names based on the colour of his skin and most recently, the nameless faceless dead man walking who'd stolen the most precious thing in his life, Ben.

'What do you want, exactly?'

But he already knew and as River and Byron laid the deal out for him, he nodded his agreement because really what choice did he have?

Chapter Twenty-Three

River was laughing as they left. He said to Byron, 'Do you like me new suit?' and Byron started chuckling, too.

'I thought he was going to shit himself, By.'

Byron wrinkled his nose, he'd had a few of those in his time – never good. 'I'm glad he didn't.'

'Me too. It is a nice suit.'

Byron grinned. 'Thanks, I got it made. Stupid really but your dad insisted.'

River nodded. 'You're proper on the firm then, eh?'

Byron's face fell. 'I didn't ask for it.'

River slapped his shoulder. 'Give over, mate, I'm not whining about it. I'm glad. I like working with you.'

Byron felt a rush of relief and again, that knowledge that he liked River. Not something he'd foreseen and an aspect of all of this he was hoping wouldn't complicate things further down the line.

'I do, too.'

'We managed that with no blood spilled either.' Byron heard the relief in River's voice.

He said, 'Better that way, isn't it?'

River nodded. 'I think so. Dad and Des thrive on it though.'

Byron nodded. He'd seen the truth of that. There had been moments when those men were bored, or in Dan's case, drunk, and he'd seen them go looking for a fight. Violence just for its own sake. Byron didn't like it and recognised that River didn't either. The truth was, Dan and Des didn't need to be involved in skulduggery anymore. They couldn't make much more money than they were without going into full legitimate business, but he reckoned both were fairly enamoured with the lifestyle. It wasn't what he wanted long-term, wasn't what he planned on having ultimately. Byron had plenty of dreams, especially since he'd met Grace, and he was determined to make them a reality even if he hadn't quite worked out how yet.

'You coming to get lunch?'

Byron shook his head. 'Not today, I've got an errand.' He added, 'Family stuff,' quickly and with an eye roll.

River nodded his understanding. 'Say no more. I'll pop sandwiches into the girls.'

'Thanks, mate.'

Chapter Twenty-Four

One of the most useful things about working with Dan and Des was the wide and varied array of contacts they came with. While Byron was up against an often poor first impression, because racism was rife and entrenched in England, he had made some friends along the way. Perhaps the most unlikely being a tame copper. He wasn't tame by choice, of course – his son had got himself into some bother with the Scott-Tylers and owed a wedge. Dan let it slide on the understanding that Glynn, the daddy cop, turned a blind eye occasionally. Which he did. It wasn't his natural position though and Byron knew that were it not for his son's stupidity, and Glynn's fierce urge to protect him from four broken limbs or worse, he'd never have dealt with the likes of Dan or Des. Byron encountered him during a drop-off of a large amount of cash for the trade of some serious narcotics, a side of the business that Dan kept well-hidden from Mae. A fact Byron knew irked River and put him in an awkward position. Glynn had been furious at how out in the open this operation was and had approached Byron, who was merely doing what he'd been told to and stated his argument, which was that they – Des and Dan – were taking the piss. Byron listened. Could see the man's point of view and more than that could see how he was held firmly in place by the short and curlies. He had no choice but to look out for his boy, though personally Byron figured him for a loser, but by the same token he didn't want his officers to look like idiots.

Byron told Glynn to leave it with him. He spoke to Dan and Des, saying the problem was that someone higher up than Glynn had gotten word and if they could just use a bit more discretion they'd definitely get away with it, whereas if they continued to be bold as brass Glynn could not guarantee it.

They'd seen his point, agreed and Byron had personally sought out Glynn to tell him the good news. The older man said to Byron at the time, 'You appear to have a good brain in your head, why are you putting in with idiots like them?'

Byron had shrugged, met his eye and said, 'Why are you?'

To which Glynn had nodded and the two men formed an, at first, uneasy alliance, that had somehow turned into a friendship of sorts in the past year. It was Glynn he'd contacted for information and that contact had led him to where he was now.

He was in a motor, nothing flash, a Volvo that blended into the background, waiting at the address Glynn had given him. He had a rough idea of the timings he needed to know and as luck would have it, the man he'd come to see was walking out now. He was flanked either side by two other men. They walked with the confidence carried only by those born into inherited privilege. Byron disliked them all on sight. They stood at the gates of the grand building they'd just left. An important place, the hub of the nation's power where decisions were made. A place Byron considered closed to the likes of him. As men like Dan and Des had known before him, trying to outrun your class in England was an impossibility. What he could do, though, was make himself as rich as he could and that was Byron's goal.

They stood talking, smoking. Guffaws spread from them to Byron's open car window. He had his head buried in a paper, but he was watching and when a car pulled up for the man he followed. So, he had a driver. Byron wasn't surprised. Des and Dan had drivers. It was the ultimate status symbol. The driver left the car at the house where he dropped the man. No doubt he himself would have to walk to his final destination or catch a bus with all the other plebs.

He followed the man to a three-storey townhouse, watched him greet a pretty wife through the wide windows that looked out onto a broad tree-lined street. Saw two children come in and go again, saw the man sit down, recline in a chair and pick up the very paper Byron had just put down.

The afternoon turned to evening then night. The curtains downstairs and upstairs finally closed at eleven. Byron waited another hour and then he crept to the car, bending down and attaching the equipment, fiddlier than he'd have liked, to the car's underneath, checked it was working and that his link would detect the thing. Hi-tech spyware, Dan had called this bit of kit, and it really was. Like James Bond stuff and with the price tag attached. Dan, ever the flash git, had ordered four and not used one. If he ever noticed this missing there'd be hell to pay, but Byron was fairly confident he had forgotten he'd even bought them in the first place. Besides, if it came to it, he'd have a story ready. Byron drove home. He knew where he was now and he wasn't in a rush. He'd bide his time and help Grace get her revenge somehow. Just thinking about her made his heart pick up. He'd missed lunch today. Wouldn't do that again but Glynn had said the man left anytime between lunch and ten p.m.

Chapter Twenty-Five

That Friday when Byron didn't come in I felt an odd mixture of disappointment and relief. I was a bundle of nerves that day anyway. Lola had managed to persuade Mae that she'd behave and was absolutely fine to sing at the bar later. I wasn't so sure. I didn't think Lola was drinking to purposefully be an annoyance. I thought she was drinking because it made her feel better, eased whatever pain she was in. That would indicate, to me at least, that she wasn't entirely in control of it.

I usually went home on a Friday. Often, I'd be the one to settle Sam so Mae could go out for a few drinks. It was time I treasured if I was honest. I loved that baby desperately. I knew why and I didn't think he was a replacement for my own daughter, no child could be that. Even if I'd still been able to have a few of my own, they wouldn't have taken her place. No one could, but there was some healing in caring for Sam, a lot of healing from being part of the Scott-Tylers. Mae had one of Byron's sisters sitting that evening though. She said she thought we could both use a night out, but I understood we were there to keep an eye on Lo. And I intended to do just that.

The pub was rowdy at the best of times and Dan and

Des held court as usual. River was there, too. When Lola walked onto the small makeshift stage a hush descended. When she started to sing hardly anyone could take their eyes off her.

She was a rare talent, Lola, and whatever it was that ailed her seemed to pour out of her mouth that night. I suspected there were few dry eyes left by the time she'd finished her first ballad and when I looked around it was as though we were all frozen. It made me smile. Mae squeezed my shoulder. 'I always forget how good she is.'

I looked up at her, but her eyes had moved from me and settled on Dan who beckoned his wife over. I watched Des move aside, making room for her, Dan pulling her to him for a lingering kiss before they turned back to their daughter.

They'd been sixteen when they met. I watched them in fascination. They were a demonstrative couple. A demonstrative family. While my dad and I had certainly been close, he wasn't much of a hugger and neither was I. I regretted that now. Wished that I'd reached for him more. Wished I'd been more grown up. Asked more questions. I took for granted he and my mum were happy but looking back I wasn't so sure. She was a beautiful woman but a hard woman, too. Her core was icy. I'd learnt that the hard way. Like molten steel she was. I wondered then what had made her that way or whether it was 'just her makeup' as Mae was fond of saying.

'Penny for them.'

I spun around. Byron. I was so happy to see him I almost reached up and kissed him. Stopping myself before I did, instead I said, 'Busy at lunch?' before I could stop myself.

He grinned. 'Miss me?'

I blushed. Lola was between songs now and a few of the older men were giving Byron snide looks. He said, 'Fancy a walk?'

'Let me check on Lola and tell Mae, yeah?'

'Alright, I'll be in the shop.'

Lola slipped off stage heading straight to the bar. She was intercepted by Dan and Mae. Her frown made me smile. As I headed over, Dan was making a big fuss of ordering his daughter a coke and reminding the staff not to serve her anything harder. I could see on Lola's face that she was furious and for a second, I thought she might just storm out. Des said, 'Magic up there tonight, sweetheart.'

And she softened, looking to Mae and Dan who murmured agreement.

I decided she was probably fine and I'd be back before close anyway.

We didn't go for a walk in the end, just settled in the shop next door. Byron was sitting casting an eye over the books, something he'd normally do at lunch. 'That idiot Roy been back in?'

I nodded sadly. 'I wouldn't serve him myself.'

'Dan says to?'

'He does, yeah.' Byron lit a cigarette, sliding the pack to me and shaking his head. 'Not good business sense. He never has it to pay back, does he?'

'Always finds it somehow.'

'Yeah, robs it straight from his wife's purse. The thing

is, there's been plenty of times he's not had it and we're running out of bones to break.'

I flinched and he murmured, 'Sorry.'

I shrugged.

He sighed. 'I wouldn't do that stuff if I had a choice.'

I laid my hand on his. 'I know.'

Our eyes met and I felt all my resolve, all of my big thoughts when I was hurt over lunch, slip away. I was amazed to find that even then, I was half in love with him. 'What would you do if it was you?'

He sighed, sank back into the chair while I remained perched on the desk.

'If I could do anything in the world right now?' I nodded. 'I'd run this place, but properly. Cut out all the shady shit. Apply for a licence for a proper place, you know, those big gambling clubs where people with proper wedge go to spend and I'd do it all above board.'

I felt my grin widen, then I started laughing and I couldn't stop.

He stood, tutted and for the first time ever looked at me with anger and perhaps embarrassment.

'Oh, By, I'm not laughing because it's a bad idea. I never would.' I stood, tugging his hand. 'Come on, look.'

He still looked pissed, but he followed me and waited while I opened a filing cabinet at the back of the office. Buried deep was my own private file which I took out then, laying its contents out for his perusal. He looked at what I had. Meticulous months of research. How you open a casino. What you need. How you get a licence. How much money is required to start one up.

When he'd gone through it all he said, 'Dan's already on it?'

I shook my head in surprise. 'God, no. I mean, I don't think it's even occurred to him.'

His face changed then a grin spread across it. 'You're telling me the girl who's got my heart also shares my dream?'

A silence then, the air fizzing with so much. All the right and good things. My stomach flip-flopping. I memorised his face in that moment, his smile imprinted on my mind forever. 'I've got your heart?'

His kiss said it all.

Chapter Twenty-Six

Lola came off stage and she was buzzing. In truth, all she'd wanted before she stepped out was a drink to steady her nerves. Normally she'd have been a few in by that point and well on her way to blissful oblivion. The past few days had been terrible and she'd realised how much she'd come to rely on a nip or two of vodka to get her through. Mae was furious and worried. Lola could see that and she felt bad. She'd be watched now everywhere she went, of course. She stepped outside, lit a cigarette and let the cool air settle on her clammy skin. There was a man there, impeccably dressed. Too much for this pub in this part of town. He approached her and she watched him warily.

'Lola, is it?' An accent, like people in films. Lola guessed he must be an American.

'Who's asking?'

He pulled a card from his pocket, handing it to her, and she screwed her nose up, trying to read it in the dim street-light: 'Magnus Raven.'

'What kind of a name is that?'

He laughed. 'One born for show business.'

'Oh, yeah?'

'Yes. Some people are just made for it all, darling.'

He elongated the 'a' in darling and Lola found a smile sneaking onto her face despite herself.

He said, 'How old are you?'

'Too young for you, mate.' She glanced over her shoulder. Dan could come out at any minute.

The stranger, Magnus, laughed. 'Gorgeous little thing that you are, and you are truly, you are most definitely not my type.'

She pursed her lips at that and dropped her cigarette, stamping a foot on it. 'Right.'

He reached out and squeezed her arm. 'Don't be like that, my dear. I genuinely meant you're gorgeous and, more than that, you're a huge talent.'

'Thanks.'

She turned to go back in.

'I'm a scout.'

She paused, frowned. 'What?'

'A talent scout. That's my job. I travel far and wide.' His arms moved to illustrate what he was saying. 'Searching for the best performers in the world.'

'Right.'

'Then I take them with me back to America and I make them into stars.'

She laughed. 'You're kidding?'

He shook his head. 'I'm not, no, and I think that you could be huge, my darling.'

She snort-laughed. 'I doubt my dad would let me go for a weekend in Southend.' And besides, she had someone she knew she could never leave behind and they were here.

'Hence why I asked how old you were.'

'Sixteen.'

'So, an adult, free to make your own decisions then?'

'Yeah, except my parents pay for me to live, don't they, so they get final say.'

'With me you'd earn more than your parents have ever dreamed of.'

'I don't think you know who my dad is.'

The man shrugged. 'I can make you a star, Lola. Think about it. My number's there, but I'll pop by again before I leave.'

She dropped the card down with her discarded shoes. She was in the small warren of rooms behind the pub, one of which also served as a dressing room of sorts. Really, it was just her with a poorly balanced mirror on crates, a too-bright glaring overhead light and a stack of dresses she and Mae had picked out together. She would love to sit at one of those mirrors with bulbs around the edges and wear dresses chosen for how they'd look under real stage lights. But she had forever for that and what she wanted most of all was her man. She wasn't giving up, not yet. Her feet felt relieved to be out of heels and she flexed them, pointing and curling her toes, rolling her ankles from side to side. She hadn't turned the glaring light on yet; it always made her eyes ache, and she had the beginnings of a headache forming already. Outside she heard someone coming. The familiar voices of her dad and Des. She stood, sliding her feet back into her shoes, and went to the door, meaning to open it and say hi, bask in their praise.

But she heard her dad say her name and that stilled her.

The room outside this one was where they all played poker and she could hear one of them getting glasses, no doubt her dad pouring him and Des generous measures because obviously it was fine for him to drink. She pressed her ear to the door.

'Mae thinks she's got her under control now and hopefully some of Grace's sensible nature will rub off on her.'

Des laughed. 'You reckon?'

'I don't know. I mean, she's had a tough year obviously.'

Des grunted, 'So she's managed to stay sober for what, a week?'

'Less than that,' Dan admitted. 'But it's a start.'

'Sure it is, but don't you think round here, being where she is, who she is, might make it difficult?'

Dan groaned. 'I know, Des. And I showed Mae the brochures you gave me – thanks, by the way.'

'No need to thank me, your family are my family, too. I just want what's best for her.'

'And you think that's getting away from here?'

There was a pause. Lola waited, her breath held. 'That's a nice drop.' Daniel. They kept the expensive whisky down here. The smell of cigar smoke crept under the door.

They were sitting out there, drinking and smoking, discussing her future as though she was a thing instead of an actual person with feelings and a heart that was literally being shattered into a million pieces by every word they were saying.

'Well?' Daniel.

A sigh from Des. She squeezed her eyes shut and felt a tear run down her cheek. 'Send her to that school, to board.

It looks lovely, for goodness' sake, like a holiday. She can grow up there in peace, away from whoever is causing the trouble down here.'

A pause. Lola's hand was pressed across her mouth, trying to keep the sobs from escaping. She was aware that she felt shaky all over, that she was balanced precariously against the door and in her stupid heels she wouldn't be able to stay still, and thus silent, for much longer.

'Mae won't like it.'

'She'll come around. Besides, you've a few weeks yet before anything needs doing.'

'I have to pay a deposit now though, if I want to secure her place.'

'Do that then. Mae will come round, she's worried about her, too.'

'Yeah, but she'll want to sort it out herself.'

'No one's saying it's her fault, are they?' Des's voice was soft, cajoling, like treacle. It made Lola's stomach turn and not in a good way. She felt sick. 'It's whoever got her into that situation in the first place. They're the ones to blame but since she won't name the fucker . . .'

'Unbelievable that she's managed to keep it a fucking secret.'

'It is, Dan. She's cunning, you've gotta give her that.'

She heard a door opening. 'Thought you two were down here. Seen Lo?' Mae.

'No, I haven't. Come on, let's go find her.'

Chapter Twenty-Seven

It was a good night. A side of me I'd presumed dead forever was awakened at the back of a betting shop in a shady part of London while my best friend sang to gangsters in the pub next door.

Byron and I got back to the pub, he to go somewhere with River, I didn't ask for specifics. Didn't want to know. He did what he had to do but he had plans and that was good enough for me. I found Mae, who had her arm around Lola. Dan was on the other side, half-cut by the look of him, telling everyone about his songbird daughter. Lola looked uncharacteristically shy. Usually, she basked in praise especially when it was her dad and Big Des, who were lavishing her with it that night.

Des left with Byron and River, while Dan walked Mae, Lola and me back. The house wasn't far from the pub and the streets between were well lit. Everything seemed to sparkle to me. The streetlamps twinkling along the Thames. Lola's glittery dress, which she still wore from singing. Her sparkly high heels, dangling in her hand, her feet firmly housed in sensible flats, caught the moonlight, her red hair swung around her waist. Mae walked alongside her daughter. A sturdier, older version. Wider hips, bigger bosom.

The ghost of Lola's future. I felt an unexpected pang for my own mother. My hand reached to the chain around my neck. Fingered the ring my father had given to her once, many years ago. I usually thought of my dad when I felt it in my fingers. Solid and familiar. But that night I thought about Nora. Comparing her to Mae, though they were a different breed, that was for sure. I liked to think she'd given me the ring to help me out, knowing that pretending to be married would be easier, or in case I needed to sell it. But maybe it wasn't that at all. Maybe she'd just been glad to get rid of the last reminder of my dad.

I watched Daniel wrap an arm around his wife, pulling her close and nuzzling his face in her hair. I wondered if my father ever did anything like that to my mother. I couldn't imagine it. Nora McCain was beautiful, imposing, but she was as hard as nails.

Daniel's arm dropped from Mae's shoulders. Their fingers found each other's and they walked side by side. I saw her turn her face up to her husband, a secret smile passing between them. No. My parents had never been like that. My father lived in a constant state of wondering if he had his wife's approval. My father, I realised, had lived for me. That had been real. What was between us. He'd loved me. I didn't doubt that.

We were at the house. Daniel and Mae disappeared into the kitchen, eyes only for each other. The door was closed but we could hear the faint burr of their conversation.

I headed up to our room with Lola. I watched her at the dressing table removing her make-up, revealing the fresh and impossibly young face underneath it.

'You were amazing tonight, Lo.'

She smiled. 'Thanks.' But I thought the smile didn't quite reach her eyes and her voice sounded heavy, distracted. I watched her now-bare face in the mirror and our eyes met.

'Lola, what's the matter?'

She paused then stood, walking over to her bag and pulling out a card. I read the name on it and looked at her. 'Who is this?'

'A talent scout, from America.'

'Wow. He saw you sing?'

She nodded. 'Says he can make me a star.'

'Lola, that's wonderful.'

She shrugged. 'Maybe.'

'Of course it is. What do your mum and dad think?'

'I haven't told them.'

I frowned. 'They'll be delighted.'

She laughed then. 'I suppose to you we must look like the perfect family.'

Her words sounded hard and fierce. The sentiment laced with bitterness. I said, 'No one's perfect.' Though my thought were that the Scott-Tylers were as close as it got.

She said, 'We probably are. As long as we all do what Dad says.'

'I think a lot of families are like that.'

She laughed. 'Not quite like this one though, eh?'

'I know your dad's businesses aren't all legit, but he's done it for you guys, so you had better than he did, right?'

'He did it for himself, maybe Mum, but he's not going to let me go to America, is he?'

'Why not?'

Tears welled up in her eyes and I went to her, feeling then like we were on the verge of something, as if finally she might share her truth. The thing that kept her up at night crying quietly into her pillow when she thought I couldn't hear. The man who she'd snuck out for, who had smashed her heart to pieces. 'Lola, you can talk to me.'

The bedroom door opened. Lola leaned forward to pick up her brush and at the same time slipped the card into a slightly open drawer on her dresser.

Mae came over, smiling at me and her daughter. 'Lola, you were brilliant tonight. Really good.'

She smiled that faint smile that didn't seem to connect anywhere. 'Thanks, Mum.'

Mae, face flushed and, I thought, slightly pissed, leaned down and kissed her head, her faded hair mingling with Lola's bright fiery mane. 'I love you, sweetheart.'

Lola gripped her mum's hand. 'You too, Mum.'

Mae gave me a hug. 'Night, Grace.'

'Night, Mae.'

Lola left the room for the bathroom and for now, that was the conversation closed.

Chapter Twenty-Eight

River sat in the shop, looking over Grace's meticulous books. He struggled with numbers, finding they moved about on the page especially if he was tired or nervous, but he could see now that every single penny was accounted for. The money that they were laundering through the shops blended seamlessly with their legitimate accounts. He couldn't fault her work and understood why Dan had started to refer to her as irreplaceable. There had also been a steady rise in profit at the shop itself and whereas prior to her arrival it really had just been run to hide other cash, now it was well on its way to being a thriving business in its own right. In some ways she reminded him of his mother. She, too, was a capable woman with many talents and a limitless ability to see what needed doing.

He could tell that Byron was half in love with her, and though she wasn't his type, he could certainly see the appeal. Lola, on the other hand, was a mess and it was barely four o' clock. She'd evidently been drinking, and River was fuming. Dan and Des were nowhere to be seen at least, a small mercy for which he was immensely thankful, but he had no idea what to do with her. Right now, Grace was trying to get her to drink coffee.

River said, 'She's well beyond that,' glaring at his sister. And then to Grace, 'How the fuck did she get like this anyway?'

'Grace isn't her keeper.'

River was about to bite back at Byron. His mood was shitty, and his nerves were frayed. Pat had told him this morning that the Salomi brothers were definitely planning something, and a lot more than trying to take over a few of their debts, but no one knew what yet. River wanted none of it, nor did Byron. They'd attempted to talk Dan and Des into handing over the reins of the more nefarious activities, going to see them before they made their first move, but Dan and Des were resolutely against it. River hated his life sometimes. Longed for some semblance of normality. His dad was a natural ducker and diver. He'd been born into a hard life and risen despite it. He talked a good talk about making it big for the sake of his kids, but River felt as though if that was true, he'd quit while he was ahead. If he stepped out now, focused on the things they could build, the shop, the pub, expanded those, they'd be fine. But Dan loved the life. That was the problem and something River had started to worry about more and more recently. He had his eye on a girl who worked in a clothes shop on the Portobello Road. A lovely, sweet thing who so far thought he was the bee's knees, Cindy Day. But she was a civilian. Came from a nice home, a few siblings, not loads of money but no one was going hungry either. River wanted to marry her, he reckoned. Could envision kids and a little house. Him working on expanding the shops, procuring business. He'd be good at it. What he didn't want was to drag her into all this shit.

'It's fine, Byron, River's just worried about her.' Grace sat in front of her friend who looked back at her through sad, glassy eyes. 'Lo, how much have you had to drink?'

Lola shrugged.

'Where did you get it?' River asked.

'The bar.'

'For fuck's sake, Lola. How much have you taken from there? He'll notice.'

Lola laughed. 'Don't worry, bro, I'll be gone soon anyway.'

River frowned. 'You're not fucking pregnant again, are you?' He himself might have a few choice words if that were the case.

'Dad's sending me away, River.' Her eyes were rolling. She was clearly having trouble staying upright and she slumped forward, over the table.

Grace said, 'Your dad's out, right?'

'Yeah, with Des, don't know where but he said he'd be a while.'

'I promised Mae I'd keep her straight.' Grace sounded worried.

River sighed. 'Byron's right, it's not your fault.'

Grace shook her head. 'This afternoon's been so busy. I was annoyed she wasn't helping if I'm honest but just figured she was out here listening to music. It's what she normally does.'

'I'll put her in my dad's office. She can sleep it off there. You ring Mae, say we're all going to eat out or something.' Grace nodded.

'Byron, give me a hand, yeah?'

She was snoring softly by the time they'd carried her up the stairs. Byron glanced at his watch; he'd told River he had some stuff to do that afternoon. River hadn't pried but had filed away that Byron was up to something he wasn't sharing with him, or his dad. He wanted to trust him, felt instinctively that he could, but you never knew. The thought was pushed from his mind as Lola rolled over and proceeded to throw up on the floor of Dan's office. Remnants of the vile yellow splashed onto River's shoes and he yelled, 'Fuck.'

The door swung open. 'I heard you down the hallway . . . oh, shit.' Grace.

Lola was dry heaving and started coughing. The coughing turned into a strangled sound. River looked on helplessly, but Grace raced forward, butting him out of the way, dragging Lola off the small, much treasured, now ruined settee and clasping the girl from behind.

She was choking. River realised it as her face started to turn blue. Grace appeared to be yanking her from behind, and he sank to his knees in front of his sister. He'd heard people say when you died your life flashed before your eyes.

He'd seen men die, watched his dad and Des take out two men before his very eyes. Executed in chilling cold blood. He'd wondered that day whether they saw everything replayed like a terrible film.

That evening, kneeling in a puddle of his sister's vomit, every moment they'd shared seemed to race around within him. He was reminded how much he loved his little sister.

He'd never been a jealous brother, had been delighted the day she'd come home. Naturally soft-hearted, looking after her had never been a chore to him. When she'd got pregnant and was sent away he'd been angry. Felt somehow betrayed by her absence.

When he'd started working for his dad, a lot of what he'd seen had shocked him. It was like a known, but unspoken, secret among them. The happiest of happy families. The family with the nice house, the car. The beautiful children and loving parents. But there was rot there underneath. The things it had taken for Daniel to drag himself and Mae up were hard things. Bad things. Violence. Murder.

Mae pretended it was all good – she was the plaster holding together the tattered flesh of a rotting wound. But the maggots were in there festering, struggling to get out. River had seen his dad's other side first-hand and somehow, despite never having spoken about it, he knew that Lola got it, too. Or maybe she didn't but she got River, and she kept him sweet and playful.

If she died . . .

An awful gargling wet sound erupted from her right before a fresh, hot plume of vomit. Then she was heaving in huge lungfuls of air and Grace was cradling her close. 'Lola, slow down, breathe in, it's OK.'

She looked up at him from wide, wet eyes. 'Riv.'

'Lola.' He said her name like a strangled cry. Grace reached out a hand for his, squeezed it in hers. The room stank, he was covered in things he'd rather not think about, and he was in shock. Grace said, 'River.' He heard it as a distant sound like an echo from far away. He thought she said it again, maybe more than once. His eyes were stuck on his sister. Picturing her as a baby, a toddler. The first time she'd tried to say his name.

'River.'

He snapped his head up and looked at Grace.

'Your dad will be back in a few hours.'

'Shit.'

'We need to clean up. I'll make a start here and get Lola sorted in the bathroom; we need bleach, is there any here?'

'I don't know, maybe down in the cellar?'

'Can you go and look, River? I'll make sure she's alright.'

He looked from one to the other. Lola said, 'If Dad finds out I've been drinking he'll send me away again.' He didn't know why, maybe the absolute certainty in her voice, but he believed her then in that second.

'Go and see what you can find, yeah?' said Grace.

Chapter Twenty-Nine

When River was seven, Big Des had caught him upstairs nicking coins out of the till. River had begged him not to tell his dad. Des had been furious. Bent down low to the little boy and yelled, spittle flying from his mouth onto River's face. It had been early in the morning, before opening. Dan had popped him and Lola in there to play while he ran a few errands. River couldn't remember where Mae was but at the time being taken to work like that with Dan had been a big thrill, huge. When he grew up, he wanted to be just like his dad and Des. A big man. A man people looked at with respect and admiration. When Des had shouted, telling River that only scum stole from their own families he'd been so scared he'd wet himself. Des had seen it and his glare had hardened.

He'd grabbed his hand. By then Lola, only four at the time, was crying too and if River hadn't been so frightened he'd have said they couldn't leave her, Mae wouldn't like it, and she wouldn't have. That aside, River hated to see his baby sister crying but in that moment, he was scared and it was so all-encompassing he was mute.

Des had dragged him behind the bar, out to the warren of rooms behind the pub itself and down a cold, dank flight of stairs, opened a door and thrown the boy into complete and utter darkness.

River had never been so frightened, not before or since. He suspected looking back that it wasn't for the endless hours he'd thought it was that he'd been left in the cold dark damp of what he discovered afterwards was the cellar, but it was long enough. Terrifying enough.

When the door finally opened, Des shouted up the stairs, 'Found him, Dan,' before leaning down and whispering, 'Between us, yeah?' River was so pleased to see light, so relieved to see Des that he'd reached out to wrap his arms around him. Des had carried him up. Dan looked relieved and slightly amused. 'Thought you'd wandered out the back door, son.' He ruffled his hair and River had forced a smile, his damp trousers clinging roughly to his thighs. 'Little bugger's good at hiding, eh?' Big Des had winked at him and picked up Lola who laughed in delight. River felt a strange disconnect between the wink and the arm grabbing. Des had thrown him roughly into that cellar and as his body made contact with the floor bruises sprang up all over him. In the days that followed he wondered if he'd imagined it, then he'd see the blossoming colours on his skin and be juddered back into the dark.

Lola was quiet then, her soft baby gaze calmly tracking Big Des who grinned back at her, chucking her under the chin, making her giggle. Dan had taken River and said, 'Leave you alone for five, eh?' but with no real anger. Then he'd realized his son was damp and River saw a quick flash of disappointment on his father's face. One he was to see again and again over the years.

He still hated it down there.

He never had cause to be there either, but the cellar was where the spare cleaning products were kept. His shame at the seven-year-old boy he'd once been, terrified, shaking, his own piss drying in icy lines down his thighs, produced such embarrassment that he had to force himself to open the door and head down the steps which felt slippery underfoot. He grappled for the light switch and almost jumped out of his own skin as the place was illuminated by the bare bulb swinging from the ceiling. Even the smell seemed to assault him, drawing him back to that day where he'd first known, understood that while Mae loved all of him, the good, the bad and the bits she saw as lacking, Dan had room for disappointment. It was never said aloud but it came out in his father's actions. Comparisons to men in the firm over the years, the latest being Byron. And, worst of all, comparisons to him and Des. Hard men. Men who'd made their own way. Who'd overcome struggle and adversity because they'd had to.

Not men like him. Soft, spoiled. Ruined by too much of everything and Mae's unwavering, tender love. He'd secretly wished his father dead on more than one occasion. His heart harboured resentments he could never speak aloud to anyone. Not even Lola. Not even after she'd been banished. Loyalty was part of the deal. Part of what made you a Scott-Tyler. Dan was the king, and they were his subjects.

Or maybe Des was the king, but he let Dan believe what he needed to.

The cleaning products were on a metal shelving unit on the other side of the cellar. River made his way across it with sweaty palms, a quaking heart and a gutful of self-hatred which seemed to twist his insides. It pushed forth into his mind a distorted, uneven reflection of himself. He thought of Cindy, the girl from the shop with her soft voice and nice manners. Too good, probably, for him. A paid thug with acid-ridden bowels and the constant, awful drip, drip, drip of anxiety. He thought of Lola, a baby in her tummy when she was still a child herself and now, tearful with sick in her hair. The sound of her struggling to breathe. He'd cry if he was capable but he'd learnt years ago how to hold in the tears. They weren't welcome from him. To Dan and Des, they signified a kind of weakness neither man could tolerate.

Lola had said Dan wanted to send her away again and suddenly River was angry. They were all pawns on the chessboard of a mad man.

He reached for the bleach, fear squelched by his annoyance and his fierce overwhelming need to protect his sister, from what he was never entirely sure. Herself today, he supposed. He stepped forward and his foot caught on something. Under the shelves were wooden floorboards, a departure from the chilled, damp concrete floor of his nightmares. He wriggled the toe of his foot, and a board came up with it.

For goodness' sake. He put the bleach back, bending down to free his shoe.

The board was displaced, and he realised it was a small trapdoor and that underneath it were objects.

He bent down and looked inside. Dark shadows made it difficult to decipher what was there. He put his hand in, pulling out what he could. Bundles of cash in unmarked envelopes held together with thick red rubber bands. He shook his head, almost amused. Their house was the same. Despite the legitimacy of most of what they did, Dan still kept 'readies' around the place. River suspected that at times he forgot where they were. Under the money was a set of keys he'd never seen before and something else in a clear plastic envelope that sealed with a finger-pressed line. He opened it carefully, pulled out what was inside and felt the contents of his stomach turn and roil.

He put everything back, carefully but quickly, his hands shaking, his eyes burning with the horror. He took the bleach and hurried upstairs, back to his sister and Grace. Wondering what to do, who to tell. Who could he trust?

Chapter Thirty

We got away with it, I think. We spent most of that day scrubbing the floor. I took Lola home in the evening, told Mae she had a stomach bug and needed rest. If Mae was suspicious, she didn't vocalise it. The next morning, I left Lola where she was and went into the shop alone. If I was honest, I preferred the days she wasn't there. She was a liability. A natural dreamer born for performing, not keeping tallies of cash in and out. She hadn't told River about the scout but what she had said about Dan sending her away swam around in my mind. She had to keep it together. Her absence would be not only a wound for Mae and River but also for me, and besides, without her, would I still be welcome?

I had the money that I'd taken from my mother's house. I'd tried giving it to Mae and she'd been appalled at the thought. I was paid for my work in the shop, too, and I'd saved most of that. I had a nest egg. One I was hoping to eventually plough into a business of my own. Or, if I was completely truthful, with Byron.

The morning passed quickly, the door went and he was there. I turned the closed sign and we settled down to eat.

'River told me about Lola.' He shook his head.

I sighed. 'It's awful, Byron. She said Dan's thinking of sending her away, too.'

'Where?'

'Some sort of boarding school apparently, she overheard him talking to Des.'

'Was it Des's idea?'

I frowned. 'I don't know, why would it be?'

Byron shrugged.

'By?'

'He makes the decisions, Grace.'

'For the business, yes, but Dan is in charge of his family, no?'

'You're probably right.' He smiled. 'I know the work side of it.'

I smiled back but that thought stuck with me. I'd noticed by then that though Mae was always very welcoming and openly demonstrative in her warmth towards Des, that sometimes it seemed forced. Lola had told me that Des and Dan were childhood friends, closer than brothers. Family in all the ways that mattered bar blood. I wondered whether she ever felt her marriage was crowded by the extra addition. Though I suppose it would have been the same way if he'd had a real brother he was tight with. Byron was close to his little sisters – would I one day resent their intrusion in our lives? That thought made me blush as I had it. Me, working on the assumption that Byron and I would be a thing in years to come.

I covered my embarrassment by getting up and making coffee. When I put the mug down, he was staring at me so intently it made me laugh. 'Have I got lipstick on my teeth or something?'

He shook his head. 'Sit.'

I was still smiling but spreading through me was a wave of nerves, too. 'You look very serious.'

'Your daughter.'

'Chloe.' Her tiny hand, curled around my finger, her face searching my chest for food. The weight of her in my arms. The pain of her absence. I thought about her less by then but still at least once a day and the vividness of it all never seemed to dim as I'd thought it would. I was glad for it. Bittersweet though the memories were, at least the cutting agony reminded me she'd been real. 'You know where she is.' It wasn't really a question. He wouldn't have mentioned it unless he knew something of importance. Byron wasn't the type to toy with emotions and he chose his words sparingly. His language and sentences were clear and concise. In stark contrast to his mother who never seemed quiet long enough to draw air if she was awake.

Byron took my hand, his fingers rough against my skin. I looked down at them intertwined. 'I know where she is and who with. Do you want to know?'

'Yes.' I didn't hesitate, didn't need to think about it.

He reached down into his bag, took out a thin file, photocopies mainly. Details of a couple who lived in the Cotswolds. The man a doctor. The wife a teacher who'd given up her work when they adopted a baby. My baby. Chloe. They couldn't have children of their own, had tried for close to a decade. They had a huge house, family nearby and money at their disposal. Tears fell as I read everything, devouring each word as though they were morsels of food and I was starving. Their surname was Betts. That was her name now, too, but they had kept Chloe. I sobbed then, heartsore and full of a heady combination of things. Byron slipped around the table, took me in his arms and held me without saying a word. In that moment, somehow I let her go. I was still to think of her often, but I no longer held the idea that one day we would be reunited. She had a home, a family. She was loved. There was nothing more I could wish for her. Nothing that I could give that she didn't already have.

When I was done Byron asked, 'Did I do the right thing?'

I nodded. 'Yes.'

'Does it help?'

'I think so.'

'We can always find her later if we need to.' We.

'Byron, I told you I can't have any more children.'

'I know that.'

I shook my head. 'You're a brilliant big brother, you've all but raised the girls and Ben.' I saw him wince when I said his brother's name and I took his hand in mine and squeezed it. 'One day you'll be a good father and with me you can never have that.'

'Grace, I've told you before that isn't an issue for me.'

'It isn't an issue now.'

'And it won't be later either.'

'You can't know that.'

He was kneeling now in front of me, sat back from where he'd been just moments ago holding me to him. There was a damp patch on his crisp white shirt, a mess of my tears.

He reached into his suit and pulled out not the tissue I was expecting but a small black box. He opened it up and the ring in there sparkled and shone. 'I love you, Grace. Marry me.'

Chapter Thirty-One

Emma smiled at the man, her face aching with the unwanted action. She couldn't feel less like smiling if she tried but this was what he wanted and what 'clients' wanted was what they got. Nina was fuming over Martha, who had screamed during the earlier part of the evening. Emma had no idea what had happened to make her cry out, but it had been bloodcurdling and as Nina led Martha through the main room apologising profusely to the animals in attendance, Emma had tried to catch her eye. Martha wasn't coping and Nina had taken to keeping her pretty much sedated during the day. She was in the unfortunate position of looking even younger than her thirteen years, which meant she was popular with one man in particular. He was large with a round, hard belly and a bulbous nose. He spoke in the same cultivated tones most of their guests did. An accent Emma would once have thought of as fancy. Now it just chilled her. Nina snapped her fingers and called Emma over. Emma excused herself to the man who, as far as they went, wasn't one of the worst.

'Yes, Nina.'

'You'll have to see to the judge since Martha has put the poor man off.'

Emma looked away. 'I'm already with J . . .'

'And you can go back to him later.'

Emma's heart sank, and she felt a wave of annoyance at Martha then. She was exhausted. Her bones ached, worse still her soul ached. If it wasn't for Ben, she'd kill herself. Had been looking longingly at various possibilities around the house. She'd seen one of their customers in the pages of a paper Nina had left lying around. He was pictured with his wife, two children. He came here not to visit her, but to see the boys who were children. The words accompanying the photo had spoken of his day job, high profile and powerful, and his numerous charitable works.

She'd read as much as she could before Nina had come in and she'd forced herself to look away. Since then, she couldn't stop thinking about it. They would never let her go, would they? Or any of them. How could they? The implications spun around her young mind. She found the weekdays almost more difficult than the Friday and Saturday nights. The anticipation of horror yet to come. The almost normal rhythms they seemed to have got into there. They were well provided for. They had clothes, food. A television and books. She spent a lot of time reading with the younger children, something her older sister had taught her before she'd left home and a skill she was always grateful to have. They had moments of fun, where they were kids, rambling around a huge house and a sunny walled garden.

Then they had nights like this.

The door opened and he lay sprawled on the bed, cigar in one hand, drink in the other. He was naked, sheets tangled around his feet. It stank in that room of shit and blood and Emma's stomach dropped to her feet as she saw the stains already on the bed and the man's spreading smile. 'Hello, little one.'

She looked at Nina who smiled at her and said to the man, 'I'm sure you two will get along just fine.'

'I'm sure we will.'

The door closed, and Emma embarked upon the worst hours of her life. She experienced pain so intense that several times she blacked out.

At some point, Nina woke her, helped her into the bathroom, cleaned her up and washed her hair with tenderness in such stark contrast to what had come before that it broke Emma.

She cried and cried. Nina got her out of the bath, wrapped her in a towel and spoke softly to her. 'You did well. It's not easy but I'm very pleased with you. You helped us greatly last night and it won't be forgotten.' They walked down one of the long hallways together, Emma hardly able to stand. Daylight streamed in from the tall arched windows. A beautiful house, she thought fleetingly as she so often did. With so much ugliness within its walls.

Nina tucked her up in her bed and gave her two blue pills offered in the palm of her hand with the words, 'They'll help you forget for a bit.'

Emma took them, sipping at the water, wincing from terrible pain, and eventually her eyelids closed and she sank into blissful nothing.

Chapter Thirty-Two

'She's not been drinking, Dan.'

He laughed. 'Give over, love – what did Grace tell you, stomach bug? And my office smelled like it'd been sterilised.'

'Grace often cleans up.'

'Not in there though, I'm happy either way.'

Mae sat down with a sigh, her mind on her daughter stashed away upstairs as she had been now for almost three days. She was depressed, any idiot could see that. She'd been OK when she arrived home with Sam, and Mae had watched, making sure the baby didn't take away all her concentration. Sam was growing into a lovely little boy, had given Mae a new lease of life if she was honest, but during the time he'd been with them Lola had declined. At first Mae had wondered if it was a sort of delayed trauma, but it wasn't about Sam. It was about the boy's father, whoever that was. Mae felt that when Lola had first come home, she'd picked up with him again, and this was confirmed by what Grace had told her. No, the cause of her daughter's malaise was good old-fashioned heartbreak and while she was currently adamantly disagreeing with Dan that Lola would benefit from time away, inside she was wondering if he might be right.

'She's upset about whoever Sam's dad is.'

'And she still hasn't told us, has she? Why the secrecy?'

'Because she knows you'll kill him.'

Dan sighed. 'Look.' And he pulled out a thick glossy brochure. Mae thumbed through it. A convent, a sort of finishing school for girls. Dan said, 'If nothing else, it'll sober her up and we can go from there.'

'What if she doesn't fit in?'

Dan laughed, 'Lola is always popular.'

'She used to be when that still mattered to her. She hasn't got out of bed, Dan, for three days.'

'I know, love. Exactly what I'm saying, we have to do something.'

'I should be able to fix this, Dan. She's my daughter. My flesh and blood.'

Dan sighed and wrapped his wife in his arms, enjoying the comfort of her familiarity as he always did. 'Mae, you're a wonderful mother, the very best, but this is beyond you. Beyond us.'

'I've failed her, Dan.'

He pulled back from his wife and looked into her worry-worn face, as familiar to him as his own. He rubbed a thumb beneath her eye, catching the first tear. 'Letting her go for a bit is the right thing to do now.'

'You said that last time.'

'And it was. She was fine when she got home.'

Mae shrugged but couldn't argue. He was right, after all.

'Des says the school is renowned for turning girls who've had a few issues around, and it ought to for the cost.'

He laughed but Mae had frozen in his arms. 'This is Des's idea, is it?'

Dan frowned. Released her from his clasp and felt his first swell of annoyance. 'It's my idea. But yes, Des mentioned he knew somewhere.'

'And why does he get more say in this than me, or Lola for that matter?'

Dan's eyes narrowed. 'He's family.'

Mae swallowed, taking in the glint in her husband's eye. Perfect was how she'd describe her marriage. She was the envy of all her friends. Always had been and for good reason. Her Dan made them a pile of money and better still, he never strayed. Almost unheard of for men in his position. He was dedicated to both her and their children. More so to her, admittedly. She was his rock, she knew that, and she kept him soft enough to be a family man. She tolerated Des these days. Once upon a time she'd have said she loved him like a brother, too, but that love had waned over the years. He stepped in quietly but firmly. She didn't like the more nefarious activities, would have liked to see them all knocked on the head years ago, and she felt she could have talked Dan around to that, but Des had wanted them so they stayed, and she still spent far too many nights wide awake wondering if her husband would come home dead or alive or even at all. She hadn't wanted River taking a part in any of those either and Dan had promised her when he stepped into the firm that he'd get the above-board jobs. She knew that wasn't the case and also that Des wouldn't consider keeping a man in the firm who didn't prove his worth with his fists. She believed that River and Byron, too, were keen to break out into the real world but were held back by her husband who, in turn, was held back by Des.

She'd learnt the hard way, though, that any criticism of Des was taken as a personal affront by Dan. Des had saved him, so the story went, from a terrible time in those homes. Whatever had occurred, and she suspected it would be more than she'd ever know, Dan felt he owed Des his life. And maybe he did. Did that mean that she did, too, though? That her children's fates were always to be decided by him?

'Mae, five minutes ago you thought this wasn't a bad idea. Now because Des is involved you've got the hump?'

'No, it's just . . .' What was it? She wished they'd talked first, her and Dan, about their daughter. 'Let's see how she goes this week, eh?'

Dan shrugged. 'Sure. But next time she ties one on, and she will, Mae, this is our action.'

Mae didn't want it. Couldn't bear to be parted from her daughter whom she loved, but she had to admit she was at a loss.

Dan reached for her again, pulled her close, knew after so many years what his wife was thinking. 'She was throwing herself at strangers, Mae, completely out of it. If we keep her here, for selfish reasons, we'll be doing her more harm than good.'

'Let's see how the week goes, yeah?' But her voice sounded weaker even to her own ears.

Chapter Thirty-Three

The only place that Harse went other than home and work in the Commons was a well-known men's drinking club in the city and a house in Mayfair. It was a beautiful and imposing place. Nestled behind black wrought iron framework and with a wall covering the back gardens, which to Byron looked impressively vast especially considering its prime location. When he visited this place, he drove himself in a smaller car than the one that Byron had discovered was paid for by the man's employer which would be the British taxpayer. He'd driven past the place in daylight hours and observed nothing much other than an errant football bursting over the high walls surrounding the side and back of the house. He'd been at a distance obviously, slouched in his car, hidden behind a newspaper. Doing his best to blend in, not easy for a man of his colour in this wealthy part of town. He hoped to pass for a driver, if indeed anyone gave him a second glance which, thankfully, no one had.

The ball suggested children. A minute or so later the front door opened and a tall, elegant woman with impeccable clothing and a well made-up, but blank-looking, face stepped out. Byron noted that rather than leaving the door ajar and nipping round for the ball, she took the time to shut and lock the door from the outside. Collected the ball, walked back and shut up firmly behind her. She looked too well dressed to be the nanny, though this kind of money probably paid employees well enough. She also had an air of authority that suggested to him she was the lady of the manor, so to speak.

He'd gone away, not yet ready to ask his policeman about the address.

Later that night he followed Harse from his house to this place and saw him greeted by the woman at the front door. Eveningwear by then, from what he could make out, a red dress. A mistress then? Another family, even. He would have liked to stay longer, taken his time, but he had to visit Pat about the Salomis who it seemed were gearing up to make some sort of move, though what was anybody's guess. He drove away, glancing back just in time to see another large black car with tinted windows enter through the gates. A wave of familiarity settled in, and he paused at the end of the street, parked up and walked back using darkness to keep himself reasonably well hidden as he went.

It was a hot night, a rare thing in England. Byron liked the heat. In his mind he had a vague idea that one day he and Grace would travel, visit countries where this climate was the norm. After, that is, they made their fortune here. He had a good feeling about her, about them. He was a careful man, not prone to impulse and able to control both himself and his desires. He'd learnt from Gladys that fools raced in where angels feared to tread. He'd known Grace for over a year now and was surprised to find that the strong feeling he'd had when he first met her, rather than dimming over time, had grown. He knew love. Loved his mother still for all the good it did him, and his sisters, though Ben would always be his favourite even just in memory. He had been hardened by his experiences, of course. No way for him not to be. But he was still open to goodness. Not something he advertised, not something that would have stood him in good stead in his line of work. A lot of his job was about engendering fear, something that didn't come naturally to him as it did his bosses. Certainly though, he was more able for it than River whom he'd seen leave some of their scenes and lose his lunch.

He felt for his friend. More than he wanted to because he suspected that if it came down to it, blood would out and if River were forced to choose it wouldn't be his side he'd stay by. He hoped that's all it would ultimately come down to. A choice rather than life or death, but Byron wanted to get ahead. Wanted to get him, Grace and his family out of the skulduggery. If that meant taking out old bosses and grabbing what they had, he'd do it. He'd rather not but if he had to . . .

The Salomis weren't the only outfit Dan and Des needed to worry about, but they were too arrogant to look closer to home. At Dan's own son who was brewing resentment. At Byron and large swathes of their own workforce who were less than happy with their heavy-handed, risky approach to everything.

He was at the gates now. The large drive was floodlit, and Byron memorised the numberplate of the black car. He was fairly certain he knew exactly who it was, had recognised the distinctive over-the-top motor straight away, but he'd double check tomorrow.

Chapter Thirty-Four

I felt in equal parts frustrated with and terribly sorry for Lola. She had sworn me to secrecy about Magnus and I knew she'd phoned him once. She said it was her back-up plan. She'd waited until everyone was out of the house and rung him.

'He's willing to collect me himself, take me to America and we can sign paperwork when we arrive. I'm seventeen now, so Mum and Dad can't make me do anything.' Lola had just turned seventeen, Mae had insisted on a party that was too young for her, all tea, cake and a notable absence of booze. I could see that Lola's heart wasn't in it but she'd smiled and made the right sounds as Mae and Dan had piled gifts on her.

Her voice held more defiance than I knew she felt, but underneath her bravado Lola was frightened.

'Lo, why don't you just sort yourself out? Stop drinking, clean up.'

She shook her head. 'I can't do that here.'

'Why not?' I almost held my breath, desperate for the answer. I felt that the key to everything, her unhappiness, the tension within the house, was hidden in the truth.

'I can't tell you.'

'Lola, you can tell me anything.'

She looked out of the window of the bedroom we shared where she'd been holed up for days, not washing or dressing, sitting miserably on the bed smoking, listening to records, songs so sad they'd break the sternest of hearts. Dan was right, she was wasting away. 'Maybe a change of scene will do you good?'

Her eyes flashed as she looked at me. 'Maybe, but it'll be on my terms not theirs.'

'Your parents love you, Lo,' I reminded her, not wanting to add to that sentence that she didn't know how lucky she was.

She seemed not to hear, put her smoke out and turned, grabbing my hand, pulling it towards her. 'You and Byron, that's a good thing. Let's talk about that, it's better than my sore heart.'

'I want you to be happy.'

'I will be and until I am, I can still be pleased for you, can't I?'

I blushed, half-filled with guilt for my incandescent joy, the pocket of beauty I'd found within the mess of the last five years. She said, 'You love him, Grace.'

I nodded, tears springing to my eyes just at the thought of it. 'He loves you, too, you know.'

I nodded. 'I think he does, yes.'

'I know he does. Anyone can see it and look how proud he is. So keen to show you off, to make it official and right.'

I said, 'I know but we're young still, Lo. It's not going to happen anytime soon.'

'A long engagement is still an engagement. It shows you he's serious.'

I nodded agreement. That was exactly what it showed and I knew that he had been hoping to make me believe it when he slipped that ring on my finger. The long engagement was at my insistence. I wanted to slow it down, despite the depth of my feelings, and his. We were new to this, new to each other, after all. I said, 'I'm lucky.'

'You deserve it, Grace, so does he. It's how it should be, isn't it? True love. Why wouldn't you want to shout about it? Why should it be a dark and dirty secret?'

'That's how it's been for you, Lo, isn't it?'

That sad, sad smile on her too-thin face. 'Tell me who he is, Lola. I'm sure I can help.'

There was a silence, thick and long. I think that perhaps she contemplated opening up in that moment, but the door opened and Mae came in, bringing mugs of too sweet tea, home-made biscuits and the waft of her maternal worry and hope. So much careful guarded hope. Sam trailed behind her, his little face brightening as he saw me. He leapt into my arms and I hugged him close. Measuring the weight of him. Imagining my Chloe who, I suspected, would be lighter but not far off. The thought didn't sting me as it once had. Didn't burn through the rotten hollow core of me. I pictured her in that big house in the Cotswolds. Maybe with a pet of her own. Definitely with two parents who loved her. A mother I hoped was as dedicated as Mae.

'You feeling better, love?' she said to Lola, with her bright smile carefully trying not to betray her worry and, in an attempt to conceal, brandishing it like a weapon for us all to see.

'I am, Mum.'

'Tummy bug, eh?'

'Must have been.'

A pause. Sam was playing with my necklace. It had once belonged to my mother. I wore it out of no sentimentality towards her but because I could still recall my father bringing it home. Putting it around her slim neck. I imagined his fingers pressed onto the clasps held there in time, pressing now onto me. Stupid, of course, but love lost, no matter the form it takes, is a hard thing to relinquish. A hard thing to have removed from you even if it was only a sham in the first place. My mother's love for me was an act. Never real. The man who'd used Lola and torn her apart wasn't giving love, he was taking. Had left scars she seemed intent on picking at. But we both mourned the loss of it even so. I was ashamed then by the fact that sometimes I still woke in the still of the night longing desperately for my mother. Clinging to the few memories I had of being a small child, graced with her attendance. I looked at them by then through a different lens, of course, but for the first decade of my life she'd been my primary carer. The person I cried for when I couldn't sleep. The person I wanted when I was ill.

Mae was staring so closely at Lola then that it was as if she hoped to see into her soul. 'Let's not let it happen again, Lo.'

Lola scoffed, 'So you don't have to send me away.'

Their eyes met, Mae's filling with tears. 'It's the last thing I want to do, Lola.'

159

'It's not about what you want, though, Mum, is it? Or what I want. It'll all come down to what Des thinks, eh?' Bitterness dripped from her words and some truth impacted Mae hard enough that red rose in her cheeks. Her damp eyes flashed anger at her daughter now. 'Just behave. Why is it too much to ask?'

Lola stood and walked past us to the door of the bedroom. 'Where are you going?' Mae stood too. Sam tensed a little on my lap, turning to Mae's unusually sharp and raised voice. I squeezed him to me, and he relaxed again, going back to the jingle jangle of my chain.

'For a piss if I'm still allowed.'

Mae sank back onto the dressing table chair, and Sam left me for her, sensing her discomfort, wrapping his arms around her neck. 'Mama.'

I said, 'She'll get it together.'

Mae stood, gathering her grandson in her arms and shaking her head sadly. 'I hope you're right, Grace, because I don't think I'll win this one if you're not.'

Evening came. Lola and I sat around smoking and listening to music. I thought about her sharp words about Des and I wondered who was really in charge. Byron had intimated that Des ran a lot of the business and I wondered then how much of a hand he had in personal matters, too. How claustrophobic it must be for Mae. I was tempted to tell her about Magnus and if it hadn't been for my musings on Des, perhaps I would have.

Chapter Thirty-Five

'They're all having affairs,' Glynn laughed, nursing his pint and grinning at Byron. 'They have money, and they have real power, worldwide international power, but they are no different from your average gangster in respect of fidelity.'

Byron nodded. Didn't point out to Glynn that plenty of the faces he'd encountered had international power, too, though more behind the scenes than these men. Byron wanted that legitimate kind of fame they all had. Knew it was a way of overcoming insecurities about things he ought not to feel that way about, but he was only human, after all. He saw a future stretching out before him where one day, he and Grace would make the front pages of the papers and for all the right reasons, too. The thought thrilled him, kept him going through the tough days, of which there were plenty. None more so than this latest conundrum. He understood Glynn's need to downplay the clout and influence of the men he had sworn to track down, capture and lock up. They instead controlled his every move. He was impotent in his own life as long as Dan and Des ran it. The worst of it all for Glynn was that his son's debts were long paid and the bonehead, for his part, had learnt his lesson and steered clear of gambling now. Unfortunately, by the time it was all cleared up Glynn was in too deep; and now he was a husk of a man, for all his bravado.

'I guessed that, Glynn, but can you find out who owns it or rents it?'

Glynn sighed, 'I can try.'

They were in a large pub in Soho. A real mixed bag by the late sixties. There were people of all colours and creeds, a few transvestites dragging Saturday night into Sunday lunchtime, some off-duty coppers and a lot of good time girls, a fair few of whom gave Byron the once-over. He ignored them. Had no interest in any woman other than Grace and never would. She was beautiful, that was undeniable, but she was smart with it and that more than anything was what Byron coveted and what he was unwilling to jeopardise, because Grace, for all of her 'leave me well alone because I'm barren' talk, wasn't half as hard as she seemed. She'd been wounded, more than once, worst of all by the ponce he was tailing, and Byron would never be the cause of any more heartache for her. Dan was loyal to Mae that way. It was one of the things Byron respected about the man who'd taken him on and probably the only thing he'd emulate. Happy wife, happy life seemed a reasonable mantra and Byron planned on making sure that was the case when she was Grace Simpson. Just the thought of her taking his name gave him a thrill. He'd found a house not far from Soho and moved the family in. He had a separate annexe being done up for him and Grace. She didn't know and he couldn't wait to tell her, but he wanted this bit of her life laid to rest first. Before the wedding and before they started on what he saw as their true path, together.

Hearing about her daughter Chloe had hurt her, of course it had – another woman raising her child – but she saw the sense in leaving well alone as he'd known she would, and it had eased her fears, too, as he'd hoped.

Byron knew he was young for marriage and commitment but he'd seen transient shitty relationships via Gladys and it wasn't for him. He abhorred chaos and always would. He also knew the value of having good people in your corner, having had a severe lack of them growing up. He thought about Ben all the time and had spent time with Glynn following every lead for every missing child in London. Sadly, they were legion. But so far, no luck. He often thought while he was laying awake at night, mulling everything over, that if he and his siblings had had just one decent adult looking out for them, Ben might still be home. It haunted him, the loss of his brother. The wrench of being parted from someone he loved so much. He wasn't going to miss an opportunity to be happy with Grace. What they had, what he felt for her and, he was fairly certain, she felt for him, was rare and precious.

Byron considered Glynn now, weighed up how to approach this and decided to trust his gut. Not only did he think Glynn would do anything for his freedom, he also liked him. Considered him to be a man who genuinely wanted to be on the right side of things. Who'd accidentally and unfortunately found himself very much on the wrong footing, through no fault of his own.

'I think there's more to it,' he said then.

'Oh yeah?' Glynn's eyes darted around the place as they always did. His job was in his blood, Byron thought.

Despite the enforced corruption even here he was eyeing up the crowd for any trouble, ready to wade in.

'I think I saw Des's car going in there, too.'

Glynn spluttered on his pint. 'Des, what the . . . and what do you mean, think?'

Byron took a deep breath, scoured who was within ear-shot, no one, and said, 'Well, I know actually. I checked the numberplate today.'

'Jesus Christ.'

Byron nodded. 'Right.'

'What's Des doing with an MP, for goodness' sake?'

Byron shrugged. 'Unlikely to be sharing a mistress.'

'It'll be high-end girls then, won't it?'

Byron nodded. 'Most likely.' And then said, 'The Salomi boys want to take them down, you know, Des and Dan.'

Glynn shrugged. 'They never make a move, though, do they? They had that poxy grab for a few of the debts and backed off.'

'No, but maybe if they don't, someone else will.'

Glynn stared at him long and hard. Byron kept that look, let the hubbub around them fill the place of the words that neither said. Until eventually Glynn told him, 'As you know, I'd not be sorry to see the back of them.'

'I do know that, Glynn, and I will always remember your help, too.' He sipped his own mostly untouched drink. For effect and camaraderie more than any desire for it.

'You think this . . .' Glynn waved his hand, 'situation at the house might help any plans along?'

Byron shrugged. 'Can't say for sure, but I've got a feeling on it.'

Glynn nodded. 'Good to know.'

They finished their drinks. Or Glynn did, with Byron saying he needed to drive back. Both men ignored the fact Glynn was driving as well and was at least three drinks in already.

They shook hands at the pub door and went their separate ways. Glynn went back to the station with the address Byron had given him to see what could be uncovered, mulling over in his mind, not for the first time, the fact that Byron was someone people underestimated. Mostly because of his colour, he presumed, but also because he had what seemed an affable nature. But there were wheels turning there. Faster and more fluidly than most. He'd told Glynn about his engagement, too, and the old copper was surprised to find himself feeling an almost fatherly joy at the news. He loved his own son, but the boy was an albatross around his neck. You hoped your kids would grow to nurture you into your old age, and in a cruel irony he and his missus couldn't rely on their kid one little bit while wet old Gladys would be well provided for in her dotage if she made it. Well, if Byron was thinking of taking over from Des and Dan, whom Glynn had never liked, never quite trusted even in their glory days when his colleagues afforded them a grudging respect, that would be good news for him. Truth was, he could do with a bit of that sometime soon.

Chapter Thirty-Six

The blond man with the soft eyes was back. It wasn't that he was kind exactly. None of them were kind but he was the best of them all. He talked to her. Treated her softly, and she could almost pretend it wasn't what it was with him. She wasn't grown up yet but she imagined if things had been different, right about now she'd be interested in things like boys. In a normal way. She couldn't imagine it now. If she had the choice, she'd never be touched by anyone ever again but nothing was her choice. This was all she had. Martha had been talking about going, whispering in the middle of the night. At first Emma dismissed her. Too fragile to cling to any kind of impossible dream. What had changed her mind was knowing that things were going to get really bad for Ben. So far, she knew he'd been in a sort of honeymoon period. Nina was reasonably kind to him and everything to this date had been visual. Wrong, fucked up like everything here, but she'd heard Nina and the ghastly man with the rough voice discussing the boys' fates and they were to be the same as hers and Martha's, only worse because they were babies. She didn't think of herself as young or a child, though she was both. Ben was different and she felt an overwhelming need to protect him, keep him from harm even as she knew it was useless.

Martha was taken out sometimes now, to where exactly Emma didn't know and had no desire to find out, but she said she knew where they were located and had planned an escape route, knew where Nina kept spare keys and just needed a gate left open.

This was where Emma had come up with her part of the plan. The missing piece. They needed help from someone else and this man who was the least cruel of them all was her only chance.

He was quick and clean as always and she made sure to act as if she was enjoying herself. Most of them didn't care about that; in fact, the judge, nicknamed beast by her and Martha, preferred the complete opposite.

He smiled at her, standing and getting his clothes on and settled.

She took a deep breath, and said, 'J,' which was how he was known to her.

'Yes, Em.' He grinned at the nickname, and she forced herself to smile back though the shortened version of her name on his tongue honestly made her want to vomit.

'I, uh, need to nip out.'

He frowned. 'To the bathroom? I'm off anyway.'

She grinned. Stood naked and stretched her arms over her head. He liked to look and smiled as he did so. 'No.' A laugh. Nervous, she found her knees were trembling and sank back onto the bed. 'Out there.' She jerked her head towards the window.

'Doesn't Nina get you what you need? If there's anything else I'm always happy to help . . .'

So, he knew they were prisoners here. The last glimmer of hope died. 'That's kind, thank you. It's, uh, more for my friend. She's been hurt.' Which was true. They were both given oral contraceptives which they took daily, Emma included, despite not even having her monthlies yet. Martha had been bleeding on and off for over a week.

'Ah, the judge, eh?' J said and laughed, a twinkle in his eye. 'Old boy does take things a bit far.'

This man was not her friend. She couldn't believe for a second that she'd considered it to be the case. Worse still, he was one of them and she'd walked into an unknowing trap. 'She needs a doctor.'

He nodded. 'I see. Well, I will definitely talk to Nina about that. Can't have you lovelies off sick, can we?'

He leant down and kissed her on the top of her head. She forced herself to smile back. 'Thank you.'

Chapter Thirty-Seven

River had been pissed off for what felt like forever. Who knows, maybe that was close to the truth? He was sick of it all. Sick to death of doing what he was told. Sick to death of the rising tension at home. He looked at Byron with his ineffectual mother and actually envied him. Gladys, bless her, was doing better than she had in years. She was still half-cut most days but now it was in a nice house which Dan had initially put the rental deposit on and Byron now covered from his wages. Byron had also got a 'mother's help', which was laughable considering the ages of his siblings. But the girl, Vanessa, who'd once walked the streets alongside Gladys, was sober, capable and grateful for the job. Byron's sisters were doing well, and Vanessa kept Gladys washed, safe and at home. Gladys was a useless lump but because of that, Byron called the shots within his family. When he was a little boy, before the cellar incident, he remembered how Dan used to crack jokes about Mae being in charge and within those four walls it had seemed to River that she was. Her word was final, she doled out the rules, the rewards for keeping them and the punishments for breaking them. Outside of the house he knew his father was respected, revered. He got a thrill out of it, of course.

What young boy wouldn't? These days he was wondering who really called the shots and why it wasn't him when it came to his own life, or Lola when it came to hers.

Lola had been drinking. Grace had whispered it to him as his sister got herself ready for her set and he'd stepped behind the pub to observe her. Seen the tremor in her step and the glassy-eyed look on her face. She knew what the outcome would be and still did this. She was sat in the makeshift dressing room looking at her own reflection. She was gorgeous, his sister. No one could argue with that. She'd grown into a woman with a face that could earn a million pounds, more even. She'd still been like a kid when she went to St Mary's and he'd been glad to see her go. Horrified and haunted by the image of her, childlike with a belly full of arms and legs. It seemed wrong. It was wrong but, like so much else, River put it out of his mind because that's what they did. He, Dan and Mae carried on as though there wasn't a colossal hole in their household. Mae keeping a low profile, Dan spreading word she was pregnant and not coping well. No one believed it, of course, especially when Lo disappeared, but no one questioned it either. They wouldn't be the first family to do it nor the last.

He was wary of Sam at first, his nephew. The boy who'd caused so much trouble just by existing. Then he'd seen Byron's plight over Ben. The lengths his friend would go to for his family, especially the dependents who needed him. He saw honour in that and figured one day when Dan wasn't there this stuff would fall to him and he'd need to be ready.

He was about to step forward, offer Lola a coffee when the door on the other side opened.

Des. River felt himself take an instinctive step backwards, retreating into the shadowy hallway. A floorboard creaked beneath his foot, but Lola was watching Des and Des had his eyes on her.

He settled on the edge of her dressing table and in the mirror River saw his back, his sister's face. He was taken back to that awful day. Locked down in the dark, his baby sister's screams following him as he went. Coming up to her in Des's arms all chuckles and giggles.

'You've been drinking.' It wasn't a question, so Lola didn't grace it with an answer.

She turned to the glass, started applying lipstick, a bright red which should have clashed with her fiery hair but somehow just lit her up all the more. She was made for bigger stages than this one.

'You're all grown up, little Lo.'

'Not grown up enough to have a drink if I want one though, eh?'

'Not grown up enough to keep your trap shut when you do.'

She laughed. Des's hand reached out and River saw his sister wince, feeling his own fists clench. He was hoping against hope that what he thought, what those pictures meant, couldn't be true. The implications would be devastating.

'Des.' Her voice was low. He leaned close, said something that River couldn't hear, but she turned, slapped him hard across the face. He grinned at her, leaning back. 'You were sweet once, girl, weren't you?'

'Saying I'm not now?'

''Course you're not now. You're well past your sell-by as far as I'm concerned and ruined to boot. Up the duff as soon as you could bleed.'

'Whose fault was that?'

He grinned and River was minded of sharks swimming around the aquarium in London. Awful things with flat dead eyes.

'Saying you weren't asking for it?'

'You never loved me.'

Des stood, brushing down imaginary fluff from his impeccable suit. 'What's love got to do with it, eh?'

She stood and the two stared at each other. River's stomach churned, hot acid mixing with a hatred so deep and gnawing he could scream. That image again of Des cupping her. Her little chubby toddler legs wrapped around his waist.

'Go to finishing school. Get yourself a fresh start. You need it.'

'Do I?'

'You do, yeah.'

'Or what?'

'Or things'll get difficult for you here.'

'If I tell my dad they'll be difficult for you.'

Des smiled. 'You reckon?'

She faltered then, hand frozen with the lipstick still open and now fully applied. Des turned and walked back in the direction he'd come from.

He'd kill him. He'd fucking kill him. Lola physically jumped as she saw her brother step out of the shadows into the open of the room where she sat. She'd had a few, and her mind was fuzzy but the reality of the situation sank in. River had heard. River knew. She stood, shaking her head, her shoulders starting to shudder. Would he be mad, would he take it out on her . . . but he stepped forward, reached for her and pulled her to him. 'Lo. I'm so sorry. I'm so fucking sorry.'

'Riv?'

She pulled back, sobering up fast. Met his eyes. Saw reflected in them her own pain. She said, 'I'm sorry.'

And he shook his head. 'It's not your fault.'

'What, that I got pregnant?' Her voice was flat. The way she felt whenever she thought about it.

He asked her, 'How long, Lo?'

She shook her head.

'Lo.' His voice was gentle, there was no anger there. Not towards her anyway. She'd been so frightened of getting into trouble, of being blamed. She and River had always been close. She adored him but she'd felt his disappointment when she'd turned up pregnant. Worried that if he ever found out, he'd never forgive her.

'You knew?'

He shook his head. 'Not then, of course not. God, do you think I wouldn't have done something?'

'It was my fault. I . . . I loved him,' she said but her voice was uncertain and so, too, recently that uncertainty had lodged in her heart.

'How long?'

'Years.' Her voice was weak and soft. Years. She had trusted Des. Thought of him as an extra father but not quite the same. She couldn't even pinpoint the exact moment it had begun. Shifted from the familial feel to a different kind of thing.

'I'll kill him,' River said.

'No.'

'No? Why the fuck not?'

'Please, River. Not yet.'

He narrowed his eyes at her, and she said, 'I've got a plan. I need to get away. Can you let me do that?'

'I'll do whatever you need, Lola. Anything you want.'

'Help me.'

'How?'

'Leave it with him. For now, OK?'

His lips thinned and there was a fierce look behind his blue eyes. Violence. All the men around her and Mae were up to their necks in it. But River wasn't like Dan or Des and she was relying on that now. She said, 'River?'

He nodded. 'OK.'

She hugged him then, sobbing with relief that was unexpected. So many years, so long she'd felt split in two. The weight of this secret pulling at her insides. Making her question everything.

River said, 'What he did, Lo, it's not right. He'll have to pay.'

'Imagine the trouble it'll cause with Dad.'

'We should matter more. You should. If that's not the case, he's no better than him.'

'God, River.'

The two siblings stood held in each other's arms, both worrying about the implications of it in different ways.

Lola felt like she could hardly breathe. She was at a point where she could take no more. As if reading her mind, River told her, 'We'll get you out. Once you're gone, I'll deal with it, OK?'

And she nodded.

Chapter Thirty-Eight

Nina listened to what the man was saying and murmured her apologies. He waved them away and she noted his neat even fingernails. Well-groomed he was and kept himself in impeccable shape, too. If she didn't know about him and his predilections, he would have been the kind of man she'd have tried to snag once. Not now, though. Men like him wouldn't want a woman like her anyway, and she was fine with that. Had been used and abused enough over the years to feel nothing but relief in his disinterest.

'I'm so sorry, sir.'

'Well now, if the girl needs medical attention I'm sure the judge can sort something out.'

Nina smiled at him. He was worse in some ways than the more robust members of this little club. He pretended to play nice. Acted as though he cared. Perhaps he even convinced himself of it. She could see why Emma had turned to him. She herself might have considered doing the same thing many years ago when she still thought escape was a possibility.

'I'll make sure, of course, that she's well looked after, you don't need to worry.' And she smiled that blank soothing smile they all appreciated. There were men here who had visited her years ago. They'd looked closely at her then, not through her as they did now. She was an attractive woman still, but she was a woman and therefore of no use here.

Her uncle had sold her to this place after he'd broken her in himself. She'd been young and frightened but what she hadn't been was stupid. The woman from back then had seen potential in her, had trained her up, taught her how to manage the house, how to scout out new possibilities. She never kept more than six children here at a time. She had files on every man who walked through the door and there were cameras in most of the rooms. She also had a passport, a bag of cash and all the documents and necessities to get far away from here quickly and one day she would. But not yet. She had a financial goal in mind that wasn't quite met and she also had a duty to find her own replacement. She'd been hopeful about Emma but despite the terrible things heaped upon her the girl remained soft at her core. Nina was molten iron inside. She had no real feelings left. They had disappeared before she had finished her teenage years, never to return. It made her day-to-day existence possible. She focused on things she could have. Money, power, influence. Here in this house where she'd been beaten down as a child, smashed into meaningless shards, she had rebuilt. Now she was queen. She'd miss the place in some ways, but she also longed for anonymity and peace. No one else's problems knocking at her door as this one was now.

Martha was the main problem, would continue to be, too. Nina usually kept them until they hit about sixteen, then she rewarded them handsomely for their troubles but not before she sat them down and made them watch.

Told them they had two choices – take the money and keep quiet or tell people and have it all exposed. She chose the clips where they were of age and looked for all intents and purposes like willing participants. It usually worked, though in the past two decades there was change in the air. The whiff of things to come. Rebellion.

Children were also harder to come by. She'd thought she'd struck gold when one of her long-term visitors had said he could find the next lot and he had, but one of the boys, it turned out, had people looking for him. That had rankled. It would be her it all came down on if it toppled too soon. Though he didn't know about the cameras, of course.

She smiled at the blond man who was tapping a cigarette from the packet, lighting it and watching her through narrowed cat-like eyes.

'As I said, Mr Harse, do leave it with me.'

'I will, dear Nina, I will.' He kissed both her cheeks and she leaned in, just managing to stop herself wincing. She may facilitate these men, but she shared none of their proclivities.

Emma woke with a start, the feeling of eyes boring into her, pulling her from the shallow slumber she inhabited these days.

'Nina?'

She smiled at her and Emma's heart felt cold within her chest. 'You spoke to Jacob.'

Her breath caught in her chest, that smile. This woman. Emma had been so seduced. So reassured. Had admired

178

her the first time they met. Beautiful, well dressed, softly spoken. And she was. Emma had never heard her shout and had never been so frightened of anyone in her life. 'Martha needs a doctor.'

Nina kept smiling as she reached a hand out and smoothed Emma's fringe across her forehead. 'Martha doesn't need anything anymore, my darling.'

'W-what do you mean?'

'She's gone, gone, gone. Just as you wanted.'

'I didn't say that.'

'No? She did though. I spoke to her because I wanted to get her side of things. She assured me it was all her fault. She'd been planning to go, she said. Had it all figured out.' Her voice was like silk. It seemed to worm its way through Emma's gut. She wondered if she'd pass out or throw up. Her insides were jelly, her body, which she often felt disconnected from, seemed to be entirely separate from her now. She imagined her soul floating high above her and Nina, above the house looking down and longing for escape.

'Where did she go?'

'Far, far away, my darling, and it'll be up to you to help me when I find someone new. Yes?'

Her smile went up a notch. Bright and disconcerting.

'But the judge, he'll want her to stay.'

'Dear Emma, who do you think I gave her to?'

She laughed then. The laugh of a mad woman. Emma watched her, blood rushing in her ears. Martha had told her about the judge. How close he'd taken her to the end more than once. How she'd longed for it and resisted it in equal measures. He'd told her once afterwards, she said, that he wasn't allowed to go past a certain point, lest he'd lose his membership. Found it frustrating and tantalising all at once. But he had said he'd like to. Longed to.

Nina left, her heels making soft sounds in the deep carpet and clicking in the hall. Emma buried her face in her pillow, wondering where her friend was now. If there was any possible way she had made it out alive, knowing, of course, that the chances were slim and in that moment all hope left her.

Chapter Thirty-Nine

River was like a caged animal, pacing up and down in the living room of the neat house Byron had rented for his family. They were all asleep, even Gladys who of late had started going up at eight and being absolutely gone by nine. Both girls had eaten, done their homework and were also in bed. Vanessa had a large room of her own. When Byron was in, which wasn't often, she tended to stay out of his way. He liked her and was glad he'd put her here. The whole thing, the house, the help, would have been perfect if only Ben were here, too.

They all missed him, the baby of the clan, and each member of the Simpson household had pondered his absence. Byron had felt on more than one occasion that if the lot of them had still been intact, Gladys may even have sobered up. As it was, she'd come to, look for her youngest son and often have to be reminded of his absence. No leads still. Just a mass of missing children all across London and Ben was in some ways luckier than others in that at least someone was looking for him. Byron still held the fragile hope that he might find his brother alive. Logically he knew it was a fool's dream but his head wouldn't let it go entirely.

Right now, though, Byron's mind wasn't on his family,

it was on his friend who was ranting and not making any sense.

He'd been in the shop, half-arsedly going over the list of people who owed them money, knowing he and River would need to pay them a visit next week. It rankled because as far as he was concerned, the answer to this problem was not to provide tick. If a man didn't have the cash to place the bet, he should be barred from doing so. It wouldn't completely alleviate it, but it would certainly halve it at least.

The truth, he'd realised, was that Dan and Des both enjoyed wielding the fear they engendered like a weapon – the weapon of late being him and River. But whereas Dan and Des felt it made them untouchable, actually it was just poor business sense and, worse than that, made them volatile, too.

Grace had left to go back to her place. There had been an argument between Mae and Dan about Lola. Lola had come off stage and left the pub. She hadn't been seen since and while Byron was certain she'd show up back at home like a bad penny Grace was worried. He'd told one of the firm to go with her to look for the girl. The last thing he wanted was Grace out walking the streets.

Now River was here obviously stewing over something. He was angry, that was clear, but something else too. Byron realised his friend was frightened. Really truly frightened.

Tensions seemed to be at an all-time high.

They'd had word from Pat that the Salomis did indeed have plans to stage some kind of takeover, would be hitting at least one of the businesses, though the problem was they didn't know which one exactly. That was a cause of stress, for Byron and River at least, who were the ones out on the street, the face of the business which was likely to get battered at some point. They were both looking over their shoulders, being extra careful. Or they had been until River turned up like this in public and drunk. Byron kept playing over various scenarios in his mind. What would he do if he was them? He'd changed all the money collection and drop-off times and had the men taking differing routes, but who knew if it was enough? He'd even attempted to talk Dan and Des into going to speak to the boys, seeing what could be arranged amicably. But they'd laughed him out of Dan's office.

'River, calm down, man, take a seat, a deep breath and relax.'

River slumped into an armchair, his head in his hands. 'Byron, man.'

'Talk to me. Tell me what's happening.'

'Des. Fucking Des.'

He shook his head, not in a no exactly, so much as an attempt to clear it. 'You need to be careful spouting off about Des, man, you know he holds a lot of power, especially with your dad.'

River laughed. 'I hate him so much, By.'

Byron stilled then, held his peace. He knew this instinctively, that there had always been bad feeling between River and Des. He also got the tense vibes from Mae as well. It was his car that had been in and out of that house and Byron knew in his heart that nothing good was occurring there. He himself didn't like Des though he'd never have said it aloud, of course.

River reached into the inside pocket of his coat, struggled for a minute and then pulled something out, handing it to Byron.

It was a white envelope, which Byron took and opened. He stared at the contents, open-mouthed. 'That's Lola?'

River nodded miserably. 'At least four years ago. Maybe six.' Byron let that sink in. She could have been as young as eleven. He carried on with the images. Two girls, one Lola, one he didn't know, a boy, and men whose faces weren't in the images.

'Where did you get these?'

'In the cellar under a sort of trapdoor beneath the shelves. There's also a load of money in there, not on any of our books.'

'Your dad's?'

'Des's.' His voice was flat. Byron's mind raced to the house. The woman at the door, smile firmly in place. Hostess was what he'd thought. Probably a brothel. This put a different, sicker spin on things. He thought about the ball in the garden. His first thought had been – children. *Oh, God.*

He stuffed the pictures back into the envelope, sliding it into his own pocket. 'You sure?'

River nodded. 'Overheard him and Lola. He's Sam's dad.' He spat the words out and Byron felt his own stomach roil. Des acted like an extra father to both Lola and River, and Byron was sure that's how Dan saw him, too. River's eyes teared up. They didn't cry, men like Byron and River. Could never be seen to be weak. Byron imagined it was Goldie or Rita. Felt the judder of pain it would cause him

184

and could only imagine how his friend felt. He stood, went over to River, took his mate in his arms and let him sob silent tears on his shoulder. He took River's pain and made it his. Something would have to be done, shit like this was beyond the pale. He and River would be united in whatever occurred, of that much he was sure.

Even though there would, he suspected, be hell to pay.

Chapter Forty

In the end, she was at home by the time I got back. Dan and Mae were arguing. Proper arguing. Raised voices and banging round. It was the first time I'd ever heard them like that, and I felt sad about it. My mum and dad never fought, but looking back I could see that mostly they just ignored each other. I'd always thought they were happy. That we were happy. It wasn't until after my father died, when everything fell apart, that I saw all that had come before differently. I suppose everyone wanted to think of their parents as infallible but the truth was they were just people, too. Good, bad, indifferent. I like to think I'd have been a good mother to Chloe, but I had the sense to understand the woman who was raising her was better equipped for it. Besides, at that point I could see my future stretching before me full of hope and new possibilities.

'I was looking for you.'

Lola turned sad eyes on me. 'They're fighting about me.'

I sighed, settled onto the bed next to her. 'It's not your fault, they're overreacting.'

'You think so?'

'I know so.'

I wrapped an arm around her shoulders. She was so thin

by then that it was painful, and I was horribly aware of her coat-hanger shoulders through the thin silk of her dress. 'I've been drinking.'

'You seem fine.'

She smiled, a rueful sort of expression. 'The key to it is always being slightly tipsy.'

'Lola.'

'I know. See, they're right. I can't stop, you know. Not here anyway.'

I let the words sink in. My mind whirred with all kinds of thoughts, the main one being that I didn't want to be here without her. As if reading my mind she said, 'You'll be gone soon, Grace.'

I started to shake my head, opened my mouth to protest. 'You will. You're going to be a married woman. Byron has plans for you both, anyone can see that. Besides, you've always had plans, haven't you?'

Tears sprang into my eyes. 'They include you, Lo.'

She hugged me and I hugged her. Taken back to two scared little girls in a cold, draughty building with Jesus glaring at us from every wall, life growing within. I'd been empty when I met her and for a long time after. The numbness of everything due to Jacob Harse was only really permeated by Chloe. But later Lola and her family found a place in my heart. This house seemed so solid and stable. Home. And now it felt like a shaky structure blowing in the wind.

'You think they're right to send you away?'

She shrugged. 'I think I'm better off not here. But listen, I need to tell you . . .'

The front door slammed, and I jumped. Footsteps on the stairs. Mae's tear-stained face appeared round the door. Lola smiled at her mother, stood up and went and hugged her. Mae said, 'Dad says you need help, that we can't give it to you.'

Lola stepped back. 'He might be right this time.'

'You've been drinking?'

Lola shrugged. Mae sighed. 'And you're hardly eating, Lo. Wasting away. Is it here, our home, have I done this?'

'No.' Firm voice. 'None of this is on you, Mum. You're brilliant and I love you so much. I love you all.'

Tears, then tentative plans which Lola neither agreed to nor argued with. Mae and I sat either side of her and we talked until our eyes were too heavy to stay open. She didn't tell us, kept her secret inside as she always had but it was already too late for that. The dark, awful past was leaking out. You couldn't ever outrun it, not really. We are all just the sum of our experiences. Mae turned in, and I fell into the kind of sleep so deep it was blissfully dreamless, which probably explains why I didn't hear her leave.

Part III

It is easier to build strong children than to repair broken men.

Frederick Douglass, abolitionist and statesman

Chapter Forty-One

The sun came up in the woodland of the grand London park. It was a cold morning but bright and as the sun rose it caught on the lake, shimmering light leaping up from the still frosty waters. Martin walked his dog as he had a hundred times before, breathing in great lungfuls of fresh, purifying air. He thought of these walks as meditation. Retired now, it wasn't half as peaceful as he'd once hoped. He'd dreamed of pottering around his house, seeing his grown children from time to time. Long conversations with his wife, Maribel. He'd known they'd grown apart over the years, busy as they had both been, he at work, she raising the children. Ever the optimist, he'd hoped it would be a chance to reconnect. Sadly, it turned out that after having lived their lives separately for decades they had little left in common. She resented him being in her space and made it clear. He wouldn't consider a divorce and nor would she but they kept out of each other's way most of the time. He was sleeping in the spare room, and most days was up and out before she even opened her eyes.

This bit of the day, at least, belonged to him. He'd got Loz for a bit of company. Maribel had a whole gang of friends and never seemed short of social invitations, though they were rarely extended to him. He went into the city sometimes, to see old colleagues, but they were still there in the thick of it and he was not. His daughter lived in Sussex now and he visited her, dreamed of perhaps moving there though Maribel wouldn't want to come and he didn't want to rock the boat. He was thinking of it that morning, though. That this place was stunning but so was Sussex and better still, filled with the hubbub of his beloved child and grandchildren.

He almost tripped on something as he was lost in his dreams which, he suspected, would remain just that. It wasn't until Loz, the little border terrier, started barking at the object that he looked down.

At first it didn't fully register. Then for some strange reason he felt the urge to laugh, though he'd never seen anything less humorous in his life.

Eventually his brain kicked into gear, and he ran, Loz trailing in close pursuit, hollering for help, someone to help, anyone, and eventually another man on a similar walk came to his aid, listened to the garbled words and they found a call box, contacted the local police station.

It was a defining moment for Martin, seeing the girl's young, broken body hidden among leaves and debris. Life was precarious. Things happened that shouldn't. He filed for divorce less than a month later and Maribel was actually rather relieved. The whole thing was so amicable that he wondered why he hadn't done it sooner and on the good days in Sussex, which were plenty, he thought of the poor girl in the park and was saddened again that she had never got the chance to follow her dreams. A thing which turned out to be far easier than he had anticipated.

Chapter Forty-Two

Magnus came for Lola in the early hours of the following morning. By the time any of us realised she was gone, she was already on an aeroplane. I found out later she'd spoken to River, who had helped her to collect her passport from Dan's safe. When I checked our room, I could see that she'd taken a few things with her, including my red suitcase which had lived under my bed since my arrival. I didn't feel devastated, though I understood why Mae was beside herself. I was pleased that Lola had gone and on her own terms, but I had the good sense not to say as much the day after. Instead, I slipped out in the afternoon, leaving Mae with Dan, Sam and the stony silence. She'd left a note for her mother saying she was safe and she'd be in touch. Dan was torn between being livid and upset, knowing the reality of what he'd caused, because it had been his plans to send her away that had forced Lola's hand, and what's more, Mae knew it, too.

I walked to Byron's. It was miles away – he'd made his home in Soho by then, the place where we would eventually settle. He liked it there and so did I, a bustling eclectic place where we as a couple didn't stick out and were instead welcomed into the ragtag community.

The house he'd rented for Gladys and the kids was nice. Always clean and mostly devoid of drama. His sisters had grown into calm young women, and he was absolutely adamant that they would see out their education.

I knocked at the door and he answered himself. It was two in the afternoon by then but surprisingly quiet inside. He said, 'Looking for River?'

And it occurred to me that I hadn't given him a second thought.

'No, actually. Is he here?'

'Yeah. Still asleep though, so is Gladys. Vanessa took the girls out for the day. I was going to come over and get you at some point.'

'Oh, yeah?'

'Yeah, we need to talk.'

I grinned, stepping over the threshold, ducking under his arm and looking back. 'That sounds ominous.'

He didn't smile as I'd expected he would and I saw then that whatever he referred to was serious.

'Byron?'

'Come on. I'll get the kettle on, then wake River.'

As the water boiled, I told him about Lola, the card from the American stranger. He nodded and looked less surprised than he might. I asked, 'You knew?'

'River said they spoke and that she wanted to get away. I don't blame her.'

'Oh, yeah?' I felt hurt by that and he seemed to sense it. 'Not from you, girl. God, everyone is sensitive today.' He smiled to take the sting from his words, but I could see he was tired and I was sorry. I felt out of sorts. The whole world seemed to have tilted one way when I was expecting it to go somewhere else. I shook my head. 'You're right. It is strange.'

He made coffee then pointed to a chair at the table. 'Sit.'

I laughed. 'That bad, huh?'

He sat opposite me. 'That day, when you saw that man in the paper.'

'Jacob Harse.'

He nodded. 'Jacob Harse.'

'You found him?'

'You knew I would.'

'I suspected it. I mean, we knew he was in London, the paper said as much.'

'It did, yes.'

'What did you learn?'

'No charges were ever pressed against you.'

I nodded. 'I figured if they had been, someone would have found me.'

'Yes, man of that standing.' That made me wince. Byron stretched across the table and took my fingers in his, squeezed then dropped them. Picked up his coffee.

'He has a wife, two children.' I thought of Chloe and I managed, 'How old?'

'Nine and ten.'

He'd been a father then, a married man. I'd been a child the night he'd pushed me back, held me down and ruined my life. Or so I'd thought at the time. I contemplated in that moment where I was, who with and decided I had somehow ended up exactly where I was supposed to be. There was no one I'd rather be sitting with than Byron. I wasn't pleased about my past. Tragedy after tragedy had taken me from one life, a good life that would have been hassle free, and propelled me into this strange and somewhat erratic existence, but I could no longer regret it either. I had love. Real, deep, proper love. That wasn't something to be sniffed at.

'Right.'

'I bugged his car.'

'What?' I laughed. 'Like in a spy film?'

He nodded. 'I guess. Dan bought a few of them, but never used them, of course.'

I sighed. He had a habit of this sort of thing. I struggled sometimes with the books due to his extravagant and often inexplicable purchases.

'Anyway. I worked out where he was going, which was to work, home and to a house in Mayfair.'

'OK.'

'At first I figured a mistress then I saw other people going in and out of it. Last time I was there I saw Big Des's car.'

I frowned. 'What the hell? You're sure?'

He nodded. He had no reason to lie and he wouldn't have anyway. Not to me. He wasn't honest in every aspect, obviously – a man in his position had to play hard and fast with the truth.

He stood, went and got a white envelope, slid it across the table to me. 'River found these in the cellar of the pub, hidden away in a secret sort of cubby hole.'

I looked at them and then I stood, ran to the sink and threw up.

He was behind me, his hands on my shoulders making

comforting, reassuring circles when River walked into the kitchen bleary-eyed, looked at us, and at the pictures scattered across the table. Byron said, 'River overheard them talking, Lola and Des.'

I turned and asked him, 'Des is Sam's father?' and as he nodded so many things clicked into place.

I got back into the house and could hear Dan shouting from halfway down the street. Inside, Mae was standing ashen-faced in the kitchen, Sam half-hiding behind her long skirt.

Dan appeared to be ranting about everything all at once, but mostly, 'the utter nerve of that girl'.

I wondered if they had been going at this since I'd left and if so, how utterly exhausted everyone must be. Dan whirled round as I came in and said, 'Oh, you're back then, are you? You helped her do this, did you?'

'No.'

He sneered, 'Really?'

'Really. I woke up this morning and she was gone.'

'On a fucking plane. To America with some fucking weirdo we've never even met.' Bits of spit flew from his mouth, landing on the table. He was red-faced, irate.

Mae said, 'You wanted her gone, what are you complaining about?'

He sank down into a chair at the kitchen table, head in his hands. 'Not like this, Mae. I wanted to help her.'

Mae reached a hand towards her husband behind his back, patted his shoulder and he gripped it. Took it to him and held it between his head and his shoulder.

'Why don't I take Sam out for a bit? Give you both a bit of space, eh?'

Mae nodded. 'Thanks, love. That'd be good.'

I thought about adding something, kind words to calm Mae but I didn't have any right then. I hoped this was best for Lola. Hoped Magnus was who he said he was and could give her all the things he'd promised but there were, of course, no guarantees. Knowing what I did by then I felt it could hardly be worse than here.

The doorbell went while I was putting Sam's shoes on. I answered to Des and forced a 'Hello,' a strained smile on my face. River and Byron had decoded this was best for now. They didn't want Des to know he was toppled, needed to work out how these pieces all fit together and worst of all, neither of them were convinced Dan would side with them against Des. I wanted to disagree, to say he definitely would, but I wasn't sure either. I'd never seen two men quite so close as them. They often seemed to communicate without words, a kind of shared shorthand no one else was privy to. And if we didn't want Dan knowing, that ruled out Mae for now, too. That was worse somehow because I had no doubt she loved her children more than anyone else on the planet.

He frowned, the perfect picture of love and concern. 'That bad, eh?'

'You've heard?'

He nodded. 'I wasn't around last night, heard just now from some of the guys at the pub. America?'

I nodded. He shook his head. 'God, poor Dan and Mae.'

My gut churned, bile threatening to head up and out. I

swallowed thickly. Sam's little hand was firmly in mine. The images in that envelope burned into my mind's eye. A boy among them. Des was Sam's father. He hadn't even looked at the lad, who studiously kept his own little eyes averted from the large man who hadn't got his nickname by coincidence.

'I was going out, thought I'd give them some space.'

He nodded, though evidently it didn't occur to him to do the same as he hung his coat like he owned the place and went through to the kitchen. As the door swung open, I saw Dan stand and Des embrace him. 'I'm so sorry, mate.'

I hurried out.

Chapter Forty-Three

The house felt horribly empty without Martha in it. Now Emma felt more weight on her shoulders than ever. Ben and Jackson were out of sorts and worse than that, Emma understood that Nina was looking for someone to take Martha's place. She had a meeting later on with the big man to discuss it and had told Emma perfectly cheerfully that actually she was hoping to expand. 'Wouldn't you like some new friends, Em?'

She winced every time Nina addressed her and the last thing she wanted was friends. The last person she'd considered to be such a thing was Nina. She and Martha had had a prickly sort of relationship, Emma desperately wanting the other girl to be tougher, stronger. She'd understood after one single night with the judge why she wasn't, though, and now she was gone Emma would never get a chance to apologise.

This life was awful. Lonely, dark, terrifying. The car crash hurtling towards Ben and Jackson kept her awake at night. She was more scared for them than she was for herself.

It was Saturday, which meant visitors, and Nina was taking extra care with the two boys. Emma's heart sank as she heard them giggling, sharing sweets and making fun of each other's neat hair and cute outfits. Nina smiled so benevolently you could have mistaken her for their mother. Emma wasn't naive or lucky enough to think all mothers were good – her own had failed to protect her, had never really taken any interest in her at all.

Nina poured drinks, offering Emma a shot of vodka which she shook her head at. Nina shrugged. 'You'll have to see both Jacob and the judge tonight, so might be an idea.'

Emma's heart sank and she took the drink. Maybe oblivion would be preferable to this, who knew?

Oblivion never came though. Emma remained heartbreakingly sober despite consuming quite a few drinks. She watched a man she'd never seen before get introduced to Ben and Jackson. Nina told him to choose one, wagging a jokey finger at him with a warning not to be greedy. Emma's heart pounded in her chest and she felt overwhelming relief when the man chose Jackson and then horror at her own reaction. Nina turned to Emma. 'Jacob and the judge are en route. You pop Ben to bed, OK?'

Emma nodded, grabbing the little boy and pulling him close to her. He giggled, 'Your hair tickles.' She had tears in her eyes as she carried him to the other side of the house, the part where they lived and didn't work. Tucked him in, told him a made-up and probably rubbish fairy story with a too happy, too impossible ending. Knowing that he may have escaped tonight but his time was fast approaching and there was nothing she could do. As she walked away from him her mind thrummed. Was there nothing? She could kill them both, her and Ben. Death would be preferable to what was waiting for him. At least he'd go innocent, untainted and untouched. The thought of doing it was like a living nightmare, but every aspect of her godforsaken life was a horror show. Just when she figured it could get no worse, it did. As she stepped back out into the main room, Nina greeted her with a new girl, dressed in too-old-for-her clothes, with the same cocky smile Emma herself had probably once worn. Emma felt sorry for her. She'd have been plucked from the same streets she herself had been or else a children's home, which was where Martha and Jackson had started out. This man procured the children who ended up here. He looked at her, met her eyes and a slow smile spread across his face. She forced herself to smile back, though her heart was pounding. Martha said he wasn't too bad, as far as they went, but she hated him deeply. He'd spoken to her when she had stood freezing and terrified on a pavement in a city she didn't know. He'd told her it wasn't safe out there for a girl of her age. Said he could help her help herself. He winked at her now. 'Emma, isn't it?' He'd 'broken her in' as he did all the new girls. She should have known, of course, what she had been taken there to do. The second time she'd met him, later on in the same evening, he'd brought Nina along and that had made her pause, was ultimately the deciding factor in her saying yes. How bad could a woman be? Terrible, it turned out. It was just more of what she'd run away from once already.

Afterwards he'd been soft, kind. Spoken plainly to her, 'That's the job, you'll see men like me. They like girls when they're as you are now, not much beyond, so this isn't a full life sentence. Play your cards right, you'll earn and be gone with cash in your pocket. Alright?' And he'd stared at her from those dark eyes and she'd nodded because really what choice did she have? She'd clung to that. The thought of it being over. Of escape. But even if she left this place alive, which after Martha she felt was fairly doubtful, she was broken now. Shattered. And if anything happened to Ben, she couldn't imagine ever sleeping a full night again.

He looked away back to what he was doing, sat at the table, counting money. He said to Nina, 'New boy up with Hugo?'

Nina nodded. 'Yes, Jackson.'

'Good. I've someone who wants to visit Ben tomorrow, a familiar face for the lad.'

Nina smiled. 'He's ready.' Emma imagined having a gun, or a knife, and inflicting great and grave pain on these two monsters.

The doorbell went and Nina stood with a smile. The big man scraped up the cash, nodded goodbye to both and left through the back door.

The judge and Jacob came in. The new girl smiled but Emma saw it wobble as the judge took her in, eyes narrowed, staring her up and down as one might a prize pony. She herself was forgotten by him and she didn't even feel relieved. She could make her mind go elsewhere now and judging by the screams that started up just a few moments later, the new girl had no such luxury. Jacob settled alongside her, leant his head towards the door that had just closed with a frown. 'Let's head off somewhere quieter, eh?'

And she went because as with everything in her life, she had no choice.

Chapter Forty-Four

I walked into the shop that first Monday morning without Lola with a heavy heart. I didn't really want to be at the Scott-Tylers' anymore. I felt like an intruder there without Lola, plus I was desperate to be with Byron properly, but I also didn't have the heart to abandon Mae just yet. She was a husk of her former self. She laughed and played with Sam, made endless cups of tea and meals for everyone but the light that normally shone out of her was dimmed. There was real tension between her and Dan and for his part, he was keeping a low profile. Out more, hoping it would all blow over, I imagined.

The lights were off in the pub. Dan hadn't come home last night, and I had assumed he'd slept there but usually when he did that he'd be up and about by now. Despite going on some extraordinary benders, he was normally keen and ready to go on a Monday morning. Dan was the face of the businesses, though I'd come to understand that it was Des who was ultimately in charge. Mae and Dan had no idea yet about his relationship with their daughter, and there would be hell to pay when it came out – and come out it would. Once a secret like that began to leak there was no stopping it. Besides all that, Des was involved in other things, too. Nothing good where Jacob Harse was involved, and I had the terrible feeling that the worst was yet to come.

I walked to the shop as I had hundreds of times before. I wasn't even close to the door when the hairs on the back of my neck stood up. I could see even from a distance that the door was open. My first thought was that Dan had crashed here instead of the pub, so despite the unusualness of it I went in. 'Dan?'

The word choked in my throat. The place was an absolute mess. Betting slips littered the floor, a few stirring in the breeze of the opening door. Pens had been upturned from their pots on the high sides at the edges of the shop.

It was a shambles.

'Hello?'

Common sense would have dictated that I turned, walked away back home, and called for help but I was enraged by then. I'd come to think of the shop as my place. A haven away from all and any madness bothering me outside of its walls. I went in. The door to the back of the shop had been hacked to pieces. Our security system was top notch so whoever it was had disabled that but you couldn't access the back offices without a code. Or a machete perhaps. I entered the code anyway, opening the forlorn door and watching as the last few chunks of it sank to the ground.

Here, it was even worse. Filing cabinets were flung open and paper debris littered every surface.

I opened the till. Empty. My blood fizzed. A week's worth of takings. Not just that, my neat ledger of who owed what for the week also gone. Those debts would be lost. I remembered quite a few of them but without that concrete proof it was a write-off. The one saving grace was that I kept the longer books, month and year overviews, back at the house.

The safe, at least, was impenetrable, though I'd say whoever was here had had a bloody good look. They'd also attempted to get through to the pub but that door was metal and coded, so at least the pub was safe.

Perhaps I ought to have been frightened. Byron told me later that I should have left, run a mile but I was so angry it didn't occur to me. I did pick up the phone, though.

Chapter Forty-Five

Byron was terrified and trying not to show it as he stood in the middle of the plundered betting shop. River stood next to him, pale-faced and wretched. He was worried about his friend who'd uncovered a terrible truth and lost his sister in a short space of time, though he felt at least the siblings had got to talk before she left. It was Lola who'd told River not to be rash and Byron was glad of that, too. Byron felt weighted by the knowledge and that had to be a mere fraction of the agony it must be causing River. He knew his friend must want Des to pay and pay heavily but as Byron had said to him, that man's day would come and it would. Overriding his concern for his unlikely best friend, though, were the various 'what if?' scenarios playing through his mind that involved Grace.

He adored her, was surprised by the depth and breadth of feelings he had towards her. If anything happened to her, he'd be lost. He was in equal parts impressed that she'd had the balls to walk straight in and terrified at the lack of care for her own safety. Part of what made their relationship tick was the respect he afforded her. He didn't consider Grace to be a member of a weaker sex. Looking at the hard lives of the women around him growing up, he had no idea how anyone could consider females anything but tough on the whole. But physically she was small. She wouldn't stand a chance against a man who attacked her and what if she'd interrupted someone doing this? He wasn't going to have a go at her, add to her worries. She looked frightened enough, had admitted to him that she'd assumed Dan had passed out in the shop instead of going home.

River picked up the phone and called home. Byron could hear him talking to one of his parents. And as he hung up, he told them, 'Dad's just in. He's on his way.'

By the time Dan turned up, Grace had made coffee and in the midst of what looked like a disaster area they were sitting calmly discussing possibilities.

Dan looked awful. His eyes were red-rimmed and he stank. River stood and Dan met his eye. The two men hadn't seen each other since Lola had left and the tension between them was palpable. Grace and Byron exchanged a look. Now wasn't the time. Byron cleared his throat and Dan turned to him. River slumped back down in his seat, glaring at the mug sitting in front of him.

'It must be the Salomis, Dan.'

'Yeah, must be. Go get that ponce Pat, bring him here.'

Byron frowned. 'If he'd known about this he would have told us.'

Dan spun on him, his face red and eyes wild. 'Fucking bring him here, I said.'

Byron nodded. 'OK.'

'And you, boy, go with him, make yourself fucking useful,' he said to River who stayed seated. 'Hard of fucking hearing, are you?'

River stood and Byron could see his clenched fists by his side. They needed to tread carefully right now and River was a man on the edge.

'River.' He turned and met Byron's eyes. 'We'll drop Grace on the way, yeah?'

Chapter Forty-Six

Ben was frightened, really scared. Emma had his little body wrapped in her arms but he hadn't stopped crying for half the morning. Jackson was nowhere to be seen and Nina and the big man had spent the morning talking in horrified, stilted whispers.

The new girl was still in bed. Emma had helped her clean up last night, settled her into Martha's old room with a heavy unbearable sense of the worst kind of déjà vu. The girl had said to her, 'I want to go home.' And Emma had had nothing to say back, had instead settled for holding the girl close to her and stroking her hair. There was no escaping here. No way out.

'I hate him, the man Big Des is bringing here,' Ben told her and that saddened her heart. He was such a sweet kid. Such a gentle-natured boy. It was being eroded here, how could it not be?

Emma said, 'You knew him, before?'

Ben nodded. 'I liked him, too. That's the worst bit. When he said he wanted to play a game with me I went.' He looked at Emma from wide eyes. Young eyes with more knowledge in them than they should have. 'He told me it was a secret, to keep it quiet. But Emma, I knew that it wasn't right, that it would get worse. Knew I had to say something.'

'Did you?'

He shook his head. 'He brought me here before I had the chance.'

'Who would you have told?'

He puffed his chest up then, lower lip jutting out. 'My brother. He'd have sorted it all out.'

Emma felt doubly sorry for Ben. She knew all about keeping secrets. Had kept her step-father's for long enough. Then, when she had managed to work up the courage, the sheer bravery to say something, it had fallen on deaf ears. Her mother's words had been, 'What do you want me to do about it?' And that was that. She didn't say any of this to Ben, of course. Ben needed something to believe in and that something was his brother.

She pressed her face into his soft hair. The thing she'd noticed they all had in common here was that no one was missing them. She had no doubt now that Martha was dead and she suspected Jackson was, too, though she got the impression that had been unintentional. She figured maybe they wouldn't be seeing that bloke again. But then again, maybe they would. Maybe Ben would. The big man had said, hadn't he, that he'd be bringing a familiar face by for Ben and who else could it be? That thought was sobering and dreadful. She also didn't think anyone would be looking for them. Even the police, if they investigated at all, wouldn't make a meal of it. She herself had visited police stations before, she'd been taken into the care of social services several times. There was no safety for unwanted children. That was the thing. You existed but not like other people.

Ben wasn't the same. He was a risk. He spoke of his siblings a lot, particularly his brother whom Emma had gleaned he was extremely close to. Despite the fact his mother sounded like a total disaster, Ben had people. Something had happened with someone in his circle. Ben was too little, it seemed to her, to understand or relay what exactly and she didn't want to push him. What he'd just told her about the man who'd be headed here made sense, though. These fuckers could hardly help themselves, was the honest truth, it was an incurable sickness. Something wrong in their make-up. But often they walked around in the world acting like normal fucking humans, managing to maintain some sort of control, she supposed, because some of the men here had wives, children, respectable veneers. A mistake had been made as far as Ben was concerned. Not as bad as some of the things she'd seen happen, but enough for him to have known he needed to alert others. Enough for the man to understand he would and that's why he'd been taken, snatched, brought to this hellhole. That's why he was here. This was in no way comforting to her because it meant that he could never be released. Of all of them, he couldn't go home. He knew too much, and he had a home to go to full of people who would ask him questions.

Nina came in and smiled her chilling smile. 'We need your help.'

Her heart sank.

Chapter Forty-Seven

Sweat trickled down Pat's head like a waterfall. He could feel every inch of the material from his clothes sticking to his body. He was in a uniform of sorts. The plastic gangster look, his wife called it, and she wouldn't be wrong. Cheap was the only word you could use to describe his suit and as such at the end of this day it would stink so bad, have absorbed his fearful body odour so deeply he'd likely have to throw the fucking thing away. He was unlucky. He told herself this over and over again, as he'd watched his mates go out into the world and progress in ways he hadn't. Even within the criminal circles he insisted on manoeuvring through the fringes of, he was a small, insignificant fish. When he was first married, his dad had given him a job in his shop. A family business, which meant he ought to have been set for life. Instead, though, Pat had gambled away first the takings, then the shop itself. His parents no longer spoke to him and in some ways he couldn't blame them. His wife, he knew, was getting fairly close to her breaking point, too. And now, here he was in front of Byron and River Scott-Tyler. Both of whom looked thoroughly pissed off. They were capable of killing him, of course. Or worse. And he'd seen the end result of

Byron's worse on more than one occasion. Didn't want it to be him.

'Was it Timmy and Mason?' Byron's voice was soft and low. It sounded for all intents and purposes as if he was having a calm chat with a mate. Pat was between a rock and a hard place. His main problem was the Salomis treated him as if he was invisible. He did odd jobs for them, running around, collecting, dropping things off. Drugs, probably, maybe some weapons though he never asked. He considered the less he knew the better. Unfortunately, he did know the information Byron wanted.

'But they sanctioned it, am I right?'

Pat didn't say anything, swallowed thickly. River opened up the charcoal-grey doctor's bag that Byron was known for carrying. He started taking things out of it, lining them up. A morbid array of sharp silver items that could inflict pain and disability. Pat whimpered.

They were in the back of the shop. The place had obviously been turned over. Pat could see as he'd been marched through that it had been pretty fucked up. Papers were strewn about, tables upturned. He still could hardly believe the culprit had had the balls for it. They'd take over eventually, that was a fact, but looking at what lay in front of River now, it would be too late for him.

'It was Bert.'

Byron frowned. 'Bert, their cousin?'

Pat nodded and said, 'Can I have a cigarette?' pulling out a hankie and mopping at his brow with it. He could smell his own body. Tangy and sharp. The smell of fear. All he wanted was a quiet life, and here he was. The worst thing about it all – it was his own damn fault. He'd had a blessed start really. Inherited a shop that did good business, married a kind woman though he'd eroded that kindness over the years with his bloody gambling. Turned his wife into a bitter nag. He took stock sitting there, petrified, but also reasoned it was too late now.

Byron reached into his jacket pocket. Pat noted the way the fabric of his suit moved. Soft and shimmering, it fit the man like a glove. Tailor made, he'd say. It wasn't just the clothes though. Byron was one good-looking fucker and he had something else, too, a bearing. He gave Pat a fag, lit it and Pat inhaled deeply, allowing the nicotine to hit him in all the sweet spots. Feeling short relief as some of the tension subsided.

'So, did the Salomis give it the go-ahead?'

Pat shook his head. 'No, actually.'

Pat had gone. River sat at the table with his hands clasped around a glass of whisky. Byron stood by the back door smoking, quietly contemplative. 'Bert has some gall.'

'He really does. I don't understand how he thought he'd get away with it.'

Byron shook his head. 'He must have needed the cash.'

'Still, he must have known his cousins would find out and that ultimately, we would, too.'

Byron shrugged. People were strange and people were stupid. There was often no rhyme or reason to it. Money made proper idiots even out of good men.

They heard the bell go on the door to the shopfront, the sound of it being locked again. Des came through to the back. Byron had called him, as he knew he'd have to. 'Alright?' Des said.

Byron nodded at him, glanced at River, could see his friend's jaw clenching. He willed him to keep his mouth shut. Stay in control of his temper.

Byron told Des, 'I sent Dave McCall to bring him in.'

The adjoining door to the pub opened. Dan came in. His eyes were bloodshot again. His normally impeccable clothes, crumpled. River had told him that tensions in their house were reaching boiling point. Grace had stayed with him for the past few nights. In the same bed, though nothing had happened in that way between them yet as she wanted to wait until they were official, as she referred to their marriage. It made him smile, though he'd barely slept a wink knowing she was just there. Had spent hours of the night awake just watching her. Her hair fanned across the pillow. He liked having her with him, not just in his bed, though that was obviously a huge bonus, but with his family. She was good with his sisters, got on well with Vanessa and didn't get in her way, and surprisingly, had struck up an easy amicable relationship with Gladys, who drove the rest of them to distraction.

Des looked at Dan with a frown. 'You OK?' His voice was gentle now. The tone you might take with a child who'd fallen and cut its knee. Dan looked at his friend and nodded. They were tight, those two. A lifetime of friendship. River had told Byron they were as close as brothers, more so even. Byron understood they'd been raised in the terrible children's homes of the forties and fifties and, having some insight into what it was like to have the state involved in your upbringing, he was sure it had been rough for both men. They'd found a way to cope, though. They'd found each other. Built an empire, but it was currently on fragile ground and Byron wondered if the last straw, the thing that brought it all tumbling down around them, would be Dan finding out that his best friend in the whole world was the father of his grandson.

He was glad Lola had got away. Felt a lot more softly towards the girl than he had done previously. He'd considered her a spoiled little princess. Someone who'd knowingly ballsed up all of the blessings that were hers by birth. Now he understood she'd been used and abused. By a man she saw as a father figure. By a man she should have been able to trust.

Des patted Byron's arm and Byron forced himself to remain still rather than move away, which is what his instinct wanted him to do. They had agreed to sit on their newfound and unwelcome knowledge for now. He imagined it was easier for him than for River, who had to go home every night. His house fresh with his sister's absence, full now of his mother's pain and the rising tension between her and Dan.

Chapter Forty-Eight

I looked at Mae and thought she'd aged just in the space of a few days. Sam wobbled around the floor, picking up the pots, pans and cutlery that Mae had laid out for him, holding objects proudly up to me. I took them and inspected each one. He was cute as a button and full to the brim with a sunny disposition that Mae told me Lola had had at the same age.

She brought two mugs of tea to the table and sat opposite me. 'How is it at Byron's place?'

'Alright, actually.'

Mae nodded. 'The girls are doing well now, aren't they?'

'They are, Mae. That's thanks to you, isn't it, for getting Dan to take Byron on. Changed everything for his family, he said.'

Mae shrugged. 'Byron's done the work, though. Dan said he'd be lost without him now.'

I smiled, my heart thumping in my chest. Byron wouldn't be with Dan forever. Couldn't be. He woke sometimes in the night, startling, loud and sudden. A cold sweat on hot skin. He told me it was the things he'd done that dragged him from sleep. I wanted him out of it all as much as he wanted to be gone. But it had been necessary. The only real way he'd had to better things for himself, his siblings.

'He's a natural grafter,' I said, forcing a smile.

Mae nodded and lit a cigarette, a faraway look in her eye. 'Hard work being married to one of them, though.'

'Oh?' I knew she meant a gangster, a face. One of the men who lived on the fringes of right and wrong. She could see and fully understand the pitfalls.

'Dan had no choice, you know.' Her blue eyes searched my face.

'I know, and look at all you've achieved.'

Mae laughed. 'My girl gone, raising my own grandson.'

'She wasn't running from you.'

Mae shook her head, a single tear escaping from her right eye. She swiped at it as she stubbed out the cigarette. 'Doesn't matter, she's still gone.'

Sam stood, came over to Mae and curled his arms around her, burying his face in her lap. I looked at his hair, the colouring so similar to his dad's. Surprised I hadn't noticed before. But why would I have? Des acted like a benevolent uncle.

'Think long and hard about your marriage, Grace.'

'I love him.' I shrugged.

Mae reached across the table, took my hand. 'Try to get him out of this then.'

I wanted to tell Mae everything. Mine and Byron's plans, what Des had done to her family, how River had helped his sister in the end. Siblings she'd raised right enough to look out for each other, her son a good man. Not just charming and affable. He had heart, loyalty. Respected what other people wanted even when he wanted something else. I wanted to tell her that none of it was her fault. But it wasn't my place. Instead, I squeezed Mae's hand back and told her, 'We'll be OK.' I knew I would, that Byron would. Though I wasn't so sure about the Scott-Tylers. Once the truth came out there would be a rip in their family that would be hard to repair.

Chapter Forty-Nine

Dave unloaded Bert from the back of his car. The man had a hood over his head and was hog-tied. To his credit, he barely let out a whimper, even as he was settled into a chair placed on a large sheet of plastic with the shiny array of tools in front of him. Byron watched him take it all in and then them. Byron and River stood in the background now, Dan and Des directly in front of him. Des was grinning like a maniac, Dan stern-faced, smoking a cigarette, flicking ash. Byron had to resist the urge to guide his hand to the ashtray on the table between him and Des. House fires had been a regular occurrence during his childhood. Luckily none that ever took hold, but Gladys had fallen asleep more than once with a cigarette dangling from her lips only to have it fall onto her clothes, the sofa, the carpet.

'Alright, Bert?'

The man didn't say anything. He didn't answer Des, but instead turned his gaze onto River and Byron.

'I'm talking to you.' Des's voice got quieter when he was about to explode. A dangerous deep burr.

Bert said, 'I heard you.'

Dan kicked out at him hard, a boot to the face. The chair snapped back. Bert went with it. Silence in the room aside

from Bert's grunts, his heavy breath catching as he attempted to recover from the devastating blow. Dan stubbed the
fag out in the glass ashtray. Dave pulled Bert back up again,
came back and stood alongside Byron. Byron could hear
his breath coming out fast. Dave was a big man but not a fit
man and Byron imagined the day's exertions were taking
their toll on him. Byron didn't like Dave. Didn't like a lot
of the blokes who worked for Dan and Des. Didn't, he had
realised recently, much like Dan or Des. Des, he would
go so far as to say, he hated. Eleven Lola had been when
he'd started in on her. His youngest sister was eleven. A
child. Des wasn't just older, he was like family to Lola. The
dynamics of the whole thing were utterly sick. Dan, he felt,
was weak. He was weak when it came to his friend which
meant he wasn't strong when his family needed him to be.
Byron also hated the way Dan treated River, just because
he wasn't a born thug, which is what he suspected Dan
wanted in a son. What Dan thought Byron was.

Truth was Byron hated violence. Even as he stood there
a witness to it and looking as calm, cool and collected as
possible. Inside his stomach was like jelly.

'You took a liberty here, Bert.'

Bert shrugged. 'Your time is almost up.'

Dan and Des looked at each other and started laughing.
Byron closed his eyes. It was a mad sound, bordering on
hysterics, but he'd heard it more than once and was fairly
shocked at Bert, who knew these men and would dare in-
vite their wrath upon himself.

'That so?'

'It is, yeah. Everyone knows what you are.'

It happened so fast and so unexpectedly that for a second afterwards everyone in the room but Des stood stock-still. Frozen in surprise and horror.

Byron came out of it first, took in what Des was holding, a hot gun. The solid crack that had deafened them for a moment and left his ears ringing where he stood.

Everyone knows what you are. To Des? Did they? If so, who was included in everyone?

Bert was back on the floor again, his legs protruding up in the air. It reminded Byron of a baby bird Ben had found. Fallen from the nest and rigid on its back, its new wings unable to carry it back up. Ben had been so upset, insisted they keep the bloody thing. And though they hardly had enough to eat themselves, Ben had given the bird bits of milk-sodden bread and one day it had got its strength, flown away to freedom.

Bert wouldn't be doing that, though. Bert was dead.

It had been expected, of course, that Bert would take a kicking, that the Salomis would have to meet with Dan and Des and probably some kind of division would be made. Byron had thought maybe by area, or business type. An uneasy alliance and one that would eventually crumble, but an alliance, nonetheless.

This, though, the murder of their blood kin over a theft that was more about show than taking anything substantial – pocket change for Dan and Des . . .

This meant war.

Part IV

The soul who sins shall die. The son shall not suffer
for the iniquity of the father, nor the father suffer
for the iniquity of the son. The righteousness of the
righteous shall be upon himself, and the wickedness
of the wicked shall be upon himself.

Ezekiel 18:20

Chapter Fifty

'A girl and a boy?'

Glynn nodded. Byron let out a low whistle.

'The girl was found by a dog walker.'

'Poor bugger.'

'Right.'

'And the boy was in the same place?'

'He was, yeah.'

'And what makes you think this has anything to do with that house?'

'It's the nearest park and I've been mulling over what you told me. It makes sense.'

Byron narrowed his eyes. He believed it but Glynn was a policeman and worked on hard evidence. 'There's something else?'

Glynn sighed. 'I shouldn't say.'

Byron leaned forward. 'There's hassle coming, about to hit your patch. Either Dan and Des or the Salomis will win. If it's Dan and Des, you're fucked. If we can get something concrete on Des, get him taken out of the picture, you're home dry.'

'You'll talk to the Salomis?'

Byron actually had a meeting with them later on but he

didn't divulge that to Glynn. No need for jumping the gun. 'I won't need to. I'll keep you out of it entirely. I'm going places, Glynn.'

Glynn grinned. 'I don't doubt it.'

'I see your position, how you ended up here, so to speak.'

'Not so different from yours.'

Byron nodded agreement. Glynn was right. He'd done what he needed to do to protect and provide for his family. The same way Glynn had.

'Has your lad sorted himself out now?'

Glynn sighed. 'Mostly. He's suitably scared but he's still unable to stand on his own two feet.' He shook his head. 'It's his mum, mollycoddles him.'

'I'm sorry.'

Glynn chuckled. 'Me, too. Kids are nothing but heartache.'

Byron smiled. He wouldn't be having children and that was fine by him. He'd always taken a parental role with his siblings, which was perhaps what made that reality easier to accept. He'd be an uncle one day, he thought, and he wanted to be a good one. Didn't want his nieces and nephews having to dig around in piles of dirt for scraps the way he had. He didn't want to be doing it for much longer and he suspected that the meeting with the Salomis would provide more information on ways out of it. If it didn't, he'd find his own. He was determined, resourceful and hungry.

'So come on, Glynn, out with it.'

The man looked down at his pint. 'The kids, their bodies showed signs of . . .'

He trailed off. Eleven or so, Glynn had told him the boy

was, a year older than Ben would have been. The girl no more than fourteen at most. The policeman looked up. 'It'd fit with that house, with Des, wouldn't it?' Byron had told Glynn his suspicions. Hadn't yet given him the photos, but he would if street justice didn't take Des out. He had to be stopped. So did that fucker who'd almost ruined his Grace's life. Going home every night to a wife and two children. The implications there weren't lost on Byron either. No one in these men's lives would be safe, but it was also unlikely that their nearest and dearest knew, or at least he hoped that was the case. He'd watched Harse's wife, going about her daily business. Her life revolved around caring for her husband and children. She also did lots of charitable work. Ironically, she was on the board of a children's charity, 'Mothers Against Abuse'. If she was in any way knowledgeable, he hadn't seen proof of it.

Byron shook his head. 'The animals.'

Glynn nodded. 'I know. There's one other thing.'

'Yeah?'

'The dead girl, her name was Martha.' Martha. No more than fourteen. Her little body showing signs of abuse and laid out to rot. 'She didn't have family or anything, not that we could find and no surname either.' Not unusual. Runaways flocked to London in their droves. It was like a beacon for kids fleeing from all sorts, hoping that the city would offer them something better. It rarely did as far as Byron could tell. He'd been glad when he started up with Dan that his businesses didn't stretch into prostitution. Had respected it even and when he'd asked about it the man had chuckled, 'My Mae wouldn't stand for that.' And he'd been pleased. Despite the more odious aspects of his job at least they weren't selling skin. A high proportion of that human merchandise was made up of girls who were hardly women, and it was a distasteful thing as far as Byron could see. Little had he known that Des had that side covered on the sly.

'We asked around about her, if anyone knew her. This one girl, Betty, said she didn't know her directly but heard a rumour she'd been poached by a man and a woman team, reckoned her old roommate had gone off with the same people. Seemed fond of the missing girl, Emma. Worried about her, in light of what happened to Martha.'

Byron took out a pad and pen and slid it over to Glynn. 'Pop her address on there. I'll have a word.'

Chapter Fifty-One

I listened to what Byron was saying with a heavy heart.

Byron sighed, sank onto the sofa. He took up most of the space on it, long legs reaching out halfway across the room. River was hunched over the table, his head in his hands. No doubt, I thought, thinking about Lola. He said, 'Do you think Des did it?'

'Killed the girl?' Byron.

'Yes.'

'No way of knowing for sure.'

'You wouldn't put it past him though, would you?' It was a rhetorical question. One we all knew the answer to. But that made it no less awful.

'I want to say he wouldn't have dared to hurt Lola but he did, didn't he? Hurt her.'

Byron pulled himself up and stood, patting River on the shoulder. 'We'll get him, man.' He sat at the table, all three of us in a circle around it.

'Mae's beside herself, you know,' I said.

River nodded. 'She blames herself. We need to tell her.'

Byron sighed, rubbed a hand across his eyes. I knew he had a meet arranged with the Salomi brothers later in the day. I also knew that he didn't want River to have that information. Not until he knew exactly what they wanted. Byron loved River, genuinely, but as he said to me, blood was always thick even when it ought not to be. While Des was a bad apple and we all three knew it, none of us knew the extent of Dan's awareness or involvement. I suspected he hadn't known about Lola and Des, hence why Des was so keen to get her away. He'd got what he wanted. That was the worst of it for me.

I'd spoken to Lola the day before, mind, and she sounded OK. Better than OK. I'd heard actual real excitement in her voice. Something that had been missing for so long I'd forgotten that what had charmed me most about her in the first place had been her effervescent personality. She'd told me in hushed reverential tones that Magnus had not a girlfriend or wife but a boyfriend. She also told me that he was wonderful. Like a kind of dad. They were recording her first record and she was off on a round of auditions for films. I'd been so pleased to hear it. Funny how things could take an unexpected turn like that. Magnus had been on his last night in London when he saw Lola sing. He'd almost written her off and headed back but he'd decided to stay on a few weeks and try her again. As it transpired, he hadn't needed to, but had been on hand and available when she was ready to go.

She'd been pushed out, make no mistake. Of her life and her family, but I was glad that it had ended up being on her terms and not Des's.

Byron said, 'River, give me until tomorrow, OK?'

'Why?'

'Let me talk to this girl, whose friend she reckons went

to the same place as Martha. The more we know before we talk, the better.'

River looked at Byron. 'I don't want to do this at all, By. It's going to kill my dad. He fucking trusts Des, relies on him. He loves that fucking ponce more than he does us.' There was a bitterness and a truth in those words. He also hadn't acknowledged what seemed to me to be glaringly obvious. I couldn't believe that Dan knew nothing of Des's predilections, which then begged the question: what was his part in it all?

I said, 'He might not after this, though.' I wasn't sure of that but the last thing we needed was River getting spooked.

'Maybe so, but it's still going to be awful, isn't it, because he'll have to do something.'

'He will, yeah.' Byron. 'Twenty-four hours. Maybe not even that, then we'll all go to see Mae, together. You're not on your own, River.'

River nodded. Byron said, 'You need to get the day's list finished.' The bets still needed collecting. 'I'll go and see this girl.'

I stood. 'I'll come with you.'

'No.'

I frowned and he shook his head. 'Normal, mate. We need everything running normally. As long as River's doing what he's meant to and you are, too, I can skive off for the afternoon.' He'd normally be with River but as long as one of them went, no one would raise any alarm bells.

River and I agreed. I said goodbye to them, both with heavy heart and hot acidic worry churning in my gut.

Chapter Fifty-Two

It was the afternoon but there were plenty of girls out and about, walking their corners. They smiled at Byron as he went past, clocking his suit and his demeanour. He was polite but gently brushed off their offers. The girl he was looking for was called Betty and was just eighteen. She would be recognisable by her height, since Glynn had said she was very tall. After asking several women, some of whom Byron wasn't convinced were actually grown adults, he was told she was home and pointed in the direction of a ramshackle pub at the end of the long, busy street that matched the address Glynn had given him. He headed in. The place was a dive. Made Scott-Tyler's look posh by comparison. And Byron supposed it wasn't a bad little place, that pub. Could be better. If it had been put into his and Grace's hands, it would be transformed but that was by the by.

This place was rotten. Everything looked filthy and it stank. No amount of decoration could bring it up to scratch either. All it wanted was demolition.

There were a few hard-looking men at the bar, and they scowled at Byron as he made his way up to it but had more sense than to open their mouths. He was obviously someone, despite his colour. They could tell that from the clothes, the swagger. Plus these men might be rough as fuck, but they were nobodies, too. There was an enormous woman behind the bar with red frizzy hair and an even redder complexion. She stepped forward, thumping two meaty arms on the bar and leaning towards him, massive cleavage swaying as she went. 'What can I get ya?'

'I'm looking for Betty.'

'Oh, yeah?'

'Yeah.'

She shook her head. 'Don't know a Betty.'

He took out a fiver, slid it across the bar. She took it, turned back to cleaning glasses and said, 'Round back, upstairs, first door you come to.'

He knocked. No answer. Knocked again. 'Fuck off out of it. I need some rest, Rosemary.'

'It's not Rosemary.'

Silence. Sounds from inside. The door opened and a face peered around. 'I'm not working, mate. I'll see you tonight. Rose shouldn't have let you up.'

He scowled. 'I wasn't after that.'

'Oh. What the fuck do you want then?'

'I wanted to talk to you, about Martha and Emma.'

The girl's face fell. She was tall, alright. Almost up to Byron's six foot but she was young, too. He could see that, though he could also see the faint frown and worry lines that would be well embedded before she hit her thirties. 'You don't look like a policeman.'

'I'm not.'

'Should I be scared?'

'I'd rather you weren't. I got your name from a copper if that helps?'

She laughed. 'Not really. They can be the worst of the lot.' Then she sighed, swung the door open. 'Come in, I guess.'

Inside he could see the place was as decrepit as the bar downstairs. It wasn't a small room though, and had a double bed, a wardrobe, a stack of books and wide windows. He could also see that someone, her he assumed, had done their best to keep it clean at least and there was a small round table with a vase of flowers on it, two seats either side.

She saw him looking and said, 'Emma always insisted on having them. Even here in this shithole.'

Byron said, 'They're nice.'

She sighed. 'Yeah.' She sank onto the bed and gestured at a seat. 'I'd offer you a drink but all I've got is gin.'

He shrugged. 'That's fine.' Taking out a packet of cigarettes, he passed one to her, lighting it and one for himself before settling into the seat. 'You two lived together?'

'Me and Emma?'

He nodded.

'Yeah. This room's awful but it's cheap, cheaper still when split between two.'

'You've not got anyone else in?'

She shook her head. 'No. Emma paid three months ahead when she left in case things didn't work out.'

'Is that how long she's been gone?'

Betty laughed. 'No, over two years now.' She shrugged, inhaled deeply on the fag. She was slim, to the point of being too skinny and in a thin nightie with ragged dressing gown. He guessed she probably scrubbed up quite well but as he looked at her, he imagined she wasn't much older than his middle sister. He was weak with relief that neither of his female siblings had followed Gladys into this tawdry frightening work. He guessed Betty had a long night ahead of her and she probably did need her sleep.

'Did you think she'd come back?'

'I had hoped she might.'

'Do you know where she went?'

She shook her head. 'There was this bloke. Big fella who'd been sniffing round some of the girls, had some woman with him which made him less intimidating. Martha went with him before Emma; couldn't blame her, she was in care and having an awful time. Anything would have been a step up. Well, so I thought.' She paused. Tears rushed to her eyes. She swiped at them. 'Sorry. The policeman said . . .'

Byron knew Glynn had told her about Martha's body being found. These girls worked a hard job together. There must be a bond there of sorts, and it was probably frightening for her. Especially not knowing how Emma had fared.

He asked, 'You've no idea where they took Emma then?' His voice was gentle.

Betty shook her head. 'She didn't even know where she was going.' Then a flash of anger crossed her face. 'She figured it'd be better than this, though, and now she's probably fucking dead.' Tears quivered at the corner of her eyes.

Byron said, 'I'm so sorry. It isn't fair.' And meant it. It was life, he thought. Life wasn't fair. The world was broken when a little girl had to run away from home only to have to run away from this and into something even worse.

'Why did she think it would be better?'

She sighed. 'I've told the police what I know.'

'Tell me.'

She put out her cigarette. 'Can I have another one?' He passed her the pack and she smiled. 'Thanks.'

He waited while she lit up. 'She was too young for this.' Byron thought Betty was too young for this. Wider than that he thought there was no one who could possibly be right for this, and he marvelled over and over again at the men who used these women's services without a second thought. Couldn't understand what pleasure might be derived from such a transaction because that was all it was to the girls desperately trying to make ends meet.

'How old was she?'

'Thirteen last time I saw her.'

Byron shook his head. She laughed. 'Not unusual here, mate, same age I was when I arrived, but she looked her age, you know? I was all developed and ready to go by then, while Emma was like a kid still, same as Martha.'

'And men still picked her up?'

She nodded. ''Course, though not as many. They are fuckers, our punters, but most aren't bloody nonces.'

'OK.'

'There was this woman who approached her, a friend of the big fella. Same one had come for Martha. Said she had a house and was looking for 'girls of her stature' was the way she put it.' Betty rolled her eyes.

'What did she look like?'

'Well-dressed, softly spoken, almost a posh accent but not a real one.'

'How can you tell?'

She shrugged. 'Just can. We get punters like that, trying to disguise things. I can see through people.' He believed she could, hoped that might at least stand her in good stead out here.

Byron asked, 'The woman wanted to be her pimp?'

Betty laughed that wry laugh again. 'Yeah, I guess, and to be fair she looked like a more attractive bet than Rosemary.'

'The woman downstairs?'

Betty nodded. Byron frowned. 'She's the landlady here?'

'Yup, and as well as paying her rent for this luxurious abode, the old bitch takes a good cut of my earnings, too.' Betty shook her head. 'I suppose it's all of our paths if we live long enough and are lucky.'

'To sell other girls.'

'To not have to lay down six times a night. However you can make that happen. Rosemary might look bad but she's just looking after herself.'

'She let me up here for fiver.'

Betty chuckled. 'She'd have let you in for half that.'

'You don't sound very angry about it.' Byron would be livid if this was his life.

Betty said, 'What's the point? It is what it is.'

'So, the woman, with the fake posh accent, describe her.'

Betty did. It was the woman at the house, he was sure of it. Which meant that Martha probably died there, and Des was involved in it all somehow and this Emma, if she was miraculously still alive, was in immediate danger. He stood, handed a wad of notes to Betty who stared at him open-mouthed. 'What do you want for this?'

He said, 'You've given it to me already.' Then, 'I'm sorry about your friend.'

'Me, too. If you ever need anything else, mate . . .'

242

Chapter Fifty-Three

The Salomis ran their operations out of a taxi rank a few postcodes over from Scott-Tyler's and the betting shop. Byron went into the place warily. Either this was a very good idea and would help give him a hand up in the world or it was a very bad idea and he may not make it out alive, but either way, he was going in. Only Grace knew about this meeting, but if anything were to happen to him, she'd let others know and also she'd take over the care of his family. It was things like this that reaffirmed to him he wanted nothing to do with this life of crime he found himself enmeshed in. It had given him knowledge though, and grit. Both things he one day hoped to take out into the legitimate business world and use to build an empire.

At the front it was all exactly what it should be. A line of cars on the pavement and an attractive girl, answering the phones behind a desk and a few chairs where customers could sit and wait. When he gave his name and said who he was there to see the girl showed him to the back. Byron was surprised at the size of it. He also felt comforted by the fact that he'd been kept on premises rather than taken elsewhere. If he himself was going to kill someone he wouldn't do it in the place that was a legitimate front for more nefarious businesses. He'd have picked a warehouse, abandoned building or somewhere hidden deep in countryside.

The girl knocked on a door and someone said, 'Come in.'

She showed him inside, simpering at the two men, one of whom gave her a wink as she left.

'I'm Tim, this is Mason.' They all knew each other by face, of course, but had never met properly. Byron was immediately struck by how similar looking the two men were. Dark hair, dark eyebrows. Sharp suits, an easy-going manner.

Tim gestured to the seat opposite the two desks that they occupied. Byron sat. They all eyed each other up and he could feel a wariness in the air. They'd be tooled up, of course, but he was glad to see no heavies in attendance.

Tim said, 'You came alone.'

'You asked me to.'

He grinned. 'I don't always get what I ask for.'

Byron shrugged. 'You probably do most of the time.'

Tim laughed, a big guffaw. Mason grinned. 'He's got a point.' The tension broke like a balloon being popped with a sharp pin. Byron found his shoulders had dropped half an inch. Tim pushed a wooden box towards him. 'Cigar?' Byron took one. 'Mason, pour us drinks.'

Mason stood up, went to the corner of the office and poured three tumblers of whisky. Byron noted that it was Tim in charge. He was the older brother, so it made sense.

They all lit up, and Mason downed his drink. Tim and

Byron took a sip each. The room thickened with blue cigar smoke. The smell was sweet and pungent.

'I'm fucked off about Bert.'

Byron nodded. 'I would be, too.'

'Did you do it?'

Byron shook his head. 'Neither me or River knew that's the way it would go down.'

'And what do you think about it?'

'I think the punishment was over the top for the crime.' Tim nodded, then Byron added, 'He should definitely have got a good kicking though.' Because robbing the shop was out of order whichever way you looked at it.

Tim said, 'That's what we'd expected, and we weren't over the moon. He did it of his own accord, though he knows we don't like Dan and Des for obvious reasons. I figured we'd get a meeting out of it and that might be a good thing, resolve some issues so to speak. I was hoping with Dan rather than Des.'

'Why not Des?'

Tim grinned. 'I think we have a friend in common.'

'Oh, yeah?'

Tim nodded. 'Yes. Glynn Portwell.'

Byron frowned, felt a sharp sting of betrayal. Tim held up his hand. 'Now, now, don't be like that. He's an extremely new friend, as in we spoke to him earlier today, and he gave us very scant information. He's indicated there'd be no more until we'd spoken to you. Hence this meeting.'

Byron relaxed again, surprised at the strength of feeling for the second he'd thought Glynn may have betrayed him.

He enjoyed their friendship, he realised. More than he'd ever expected to.

'How did you come into contact with him?'

'That's the interesting thing here. We run a few houses, for men who like to let off steam.'

'Brothels.'

Tim shrugged. 'Sure. Anyway, we have one girl who turned up fairly young, but legal mind.' That grin again.

'OK.'

'She came with a long-term client, a well-known man. A respectable man. His tastes were for the younger girls.'

'Great.'

Tim shook his head. 'Don't take that tone. As I said, we run a place where men can let off steam, but all of the women we have working there are, in fact, women.'

'Even if they're barely legal.'

'Barely isn't the same as underage.'

Byron took a sip of his drink, imagining himself swallowing down a sharp retort as a way of avoiding causing trouble here. He managed, 'OK.'

'This girl was approached by a woman while she was still out on the streets.'

'Oh, yeah?' Byron forced a flat tone to his voice, not wishing to bely his obvious interest.

'Yeah, and this is the bit our mutual friend thought might interest you.'

'Go on.'

'I'll stop beating around the bush, shall I?'

'I wish you would.'

That chuckle again. Mason, speaking for the first time,

said, 'Des has been seen out and about with that same woman. Des has a reputation. He and Dan aren't liked at all in that trade.'

'The sex trade?'

Mason nodded. Byron hated that entire arm of business. 'Dan and Des don't run any of that, though, do they? That's one area you dominate, no?'

Tim smiled. He had sharp even teeth that were very white. 'We do, but Des has been catering very discreetly to that portion of the market for whom barely just isn't enough, hence his liaison with the kiddie snatcher woman. Do you understand what I'm saying?'

'I do.' Byron knew all of this but it was interesting to discover other people knew, too.

'They have more enemies than they realise.'

'Paving the way for you to take them out?'

'Exactly.'

'You want to make sure I don't stand in your way?'

'We do want that, yes. Also, having someone on their side who knows their movements . . .'

'Dan has been good to me.'

'But he is not a good man.'

'Des is the problem, though, isn't he?'

'They come as a package.'

'I don't know.'

Tim sat back. 'Take twenty-four hours, do some digging of your own, focus on Dan. I'll let my people know they must speak to you if your paths lead you to any of our concerns.'

'Will they?'

Tim shrugged. 'We don't deal in children, as I've said but we have girls who may have started out young with other people. Feel free to speak to them and also ask if they are happy with their working arrangements. We are good employers.'

'I don't want to work for you.'

Tim raised an eyebrow. 'A shame, but it's not a necessary part of this deal. What do you want?'

'To set up a real business, on my own.'

'Like what?'

'A casino.'

'That'll take a fair bit of start-up money.'

'It will, yeah.'

'Help us end Dan and Des's reign and we'll make sure you have the lump sum you need.'

'Let me think about it.'

Tim nodded. 'I will.'

They shook hands. Byron left and felt the fresh air hit his face as he stepped out. Dan and Des were done for. That was a simple fact. If he didn't know about Des he would have moved heaven and earth for a different ending. He had no qualms about taking Des down, would happily do it himself but as he'd told Tim, Dan had been good to him. He was River's dad. He needed to talk to Grace.

Chapter Fifty-Four

River picked up the phone and felt a rush of pleasure when he heard his sister's voice.

'Lo, how are you?'

'Honestly, I'm good. Great even. I've had a load of auditions, for a film.'

'No way.'

She giggled.

'Is that guy . . .?'

'Magnus?'

'Yeah, he's not . . .'

She laughed. 'He's gay, River. Has a long-term boyfriend. I'm of absolutely no interest to him whatsoever. In that regard at least.'

River didn't know how to respond to that but he was glad she sounded happy at least.

She said, 'I'm living with them. They've got this ridiculous house, like a mansion. It's got its own pool.'

'No way.'

'Honest to God, and the sun always shines here.'

'I'm happy for you, Lola.'

She sighed. 'Me, too, but I'm sorry for the way everything happened, and I miss you guys.'

'We miss you, too.' He swallowed thickly, a lump in his throat.

'You'll have to come and visit, River.'

'You're not coming back, are you?'

There was a pause, a silence that was too long. When she spoke again her voice was uneven and he realised she was crying. 'I don't think I can, River. I don't think I can ever see him again.' River felt a swell of hate. It shouldn't be her halfway around the world. Why should she have had to run?

He asked, 'What about Mum?'

'How is she?'

'She's sad, Lo.'

'God.'

'It's not fair.'

'I know.'

'I'm glad you're happy but I'm sorry you're gone.'

'I feel the same.'

'Lo, how old were you, when it started? With Des.' He looked over his shoulder, knew Mae was out with Sam, but the poisonous secret was so close to slipping out, breaking into their world when said aloud and smashing it to pieces.

A silence. He'd asked her this the other day but she hadn't given him a direct answer. He wondered now if he should just leave it. But he felt like now it was out he had to know everything. Even if it hurt, even if it felt like too much to take. Because no matter how much it might sting his feelings, what had gone on had stained his sister's soul, and he hadn't protected her, hadn't even realised.

Finally, she said, 'I don't know, exactly. We'd always

been . . . close, I guess. The first time it crossed to something else I was maybe ten or so.' He thought back to that day Des had locked him in the cellar. Coming back up, his piss dried cold in his trousers, Des clutching Lola to him, tickling under her chin, making her laugh. He'd been preparing her for it her whole life. His best friend's daughter.

'Fuck.'

'I'm sorry, River.'

'It's not your fault.'

'I thought we were in love.'

'You were a child.'

'I know. I can sort of see it now that I'm not there.' She sighed. 'Magnus has made me go to a therapist, would you believe?'

'What, like a psychiatrist?'

'Yes.'

'Does it help?'

'Yes, I think so. I'm starting to see things more clearly now.'

'That's good.' Then, 'I love you.'

'I love you, too. I'll call again, we'll get you out here.'

'I'd like that.'

After he had hung up, he stood stock-still staring at the phone as if willing his little sister home. It was a selfish thing to want, though – she was better left where she was. This was Des's fault and Dan's error for bringing that vile man into their lives. He put his coat on and left the house with steely determination.

251

Chapter Fifty-Five

'You look awful.'

Byron smiled faintly at me. 'Thanks.'

'Sorry. I just mean . . .'

He shook his head. 'It's OK.'

'I'm glad to see you.' I could hear a million fears clamouring in those words. It was an understatement. I'd been a mess all day. I knew he was going to find Martha's friend and then to the Salomis and the entire time he'd been gone I'd had visions of him turning up dead or not turning up at all.

I sat him at the kitchen table in the warm, cosy house he'd provided for the family I was becoming a part of.

He told me the day's events. I said to him, 'We have to get River and we have to talk to Mae.'

He nodded. 'I know.'

We knocked on the door of the Scott-Tyler's and Mae answered. She looked dreadful, her red hair a tangled mess, her eyes wild. 'He's not with you?'

'Who?' I frowned.

'River. He hasn't collected any of his debts this afternoon and no one's seen him.'

Byron and I exchanged a look.

'What, what do you know?'

'Is Dan here?' I asked her.

'No. He's out looking for River. Come in, for fuck's sake, it's freezing.'

She sat at the kitchen table smoking endless cigarettes, her leg jiggling. Sam had deposited himself in my lap and was sitting chewing on a rattle, dribble trailing from his lips in long stringy lines. Mae murmured, 'Teething,' pressing her spare hand to his cheek and giving the red-faced toddler a faint smile.

Byron boiled the kettle, making us all tea and bringing it to the table.

'I couldn't bear to lose both of them. I can't lose both of them.'

'You won't,' I told her, though by that stage I was just as worried. River should have finished up collecting by then and been back with us.

Mae said to Byron as he sat, 'Why weren't you collecting with him?'

Byron looked at me, I stared back.

'Will you two fucking stop it and just tell me what the hell's going on?'

I took a deep breath in. 'Des is Sam's father.'

The child looked up at the mention of his name. Mae stared at me wide-eyed. I could hear the tap dripping at the sink. The sound of Sam's snotty breath. The silent and devastating impact of four words I'd delivered quietly.

'Des . . .'

Her voice trailed off as she looked at the plump child. He

reached across the table for her, and she watched his hand but didn't reach back for it. She shook her head. 'Does Dan know?'

'We don't think so.'

'River?'

I nodded. She leaned forward with a groan, her head resting on her hands.

'How long, how old?' The implications seemed to overwhelm her and she spoke again before either of us could answer. 'She was fourteen when she fell. Fourteen. He's a grown man. My baby.'

'I'm sorry, Mae.'

'Why didn't she tell me?'

'He told her not to.'

She laughed a caustic sound. 'I bet he did. Fuck.'

She shouted the last word so loudly Sam jumped. She never raised her voice, not really and certainly not around the children. He started to cry and reached for her. 'Mama.'

She stared at him, and I saw a faint prickling of horror on her face. I said, 'He's still Lola's baby. Your grandson.'

She looked at me, pale-faced. 'But he's his son, too.'

'Mae.'

'Mama.' Sam was tearful now.

I said, 'Mae, Lola is gone, and she's alright. She's trusted you with him. Her boy.'

She looked from me to Byron, to the little one who was staring at her, reaching for her. She seemed to give herself a shake then reached for the boy who clambered off me over the table and into her arms. 'I'm here, baby. It's OK.' To me and Byron, 'It's not his fault, is it?'

'No.'

'He can never know. I don't want him to know.'

'He won't, Mae.'

Byron said, his voice gentle, 'There's something else, Mae.'

She looked at him. 'Nothing can be worse than this, surely.'

I took her hand, damp from swiping at her tears. 'That girl found in the woods, you know, in the park.'

She frowned and I said, 'We talked about it a few days ago.'

She nodded. 'That's right, and the little boy there, too.' She shook her head. 'Awful.'

My heart hammered in my chest. I loved her. She'd been kinder to me than my own mother ever had. She didn't deserve to be dragged into this mess any more than Lola had or the children whose bodies had been left to rot in plain sight. I spoke in a stilted wobble, hating the sound of my own voice, the news it had to deliver like blows across her face. Byron pitched in with details, about the house. The policeman. The things that we had pieced together and suspected to be true. He didn't mention the Salomis but said vaguely that he felt Des's antics were more widely known than we'd guessed.

When he'd finished she was dry-eyed. Sam curled up asleep on her lap, his head resting against her stomach. 'Everyone else knew, is that what you're saying?'

Byron shook his head. 'Not everyone, a few people.'

'What are you going to do?'

We were saved from answering by the front door going.

I leaned over, took her hand and whispered, 'Can we keep it to us, just for now?'

She nodded.

Dan came into the kitchen. Mae said, 'Found him?'

Dan shook his head. He sat heavily at the table and reached for the box of cigarettes in the middle, lighting one. To Mae, 'Get me a drink, love.'

I stood. 'I'll take Sam up then we'll get going.'

Chapter Fifty-Six

Mae watched her husband. Everything about home was as familiar to her as she was herself. They were kids really when they'd met. They had grown up alongside each other. She was strong in ways he wasn't, she'd always known that. And that Dan was damaged. Things had happened to him when he was a kid that he could barely speak about even now all these years later. He still came to sometimes in the middle of the night fighting himself awake. Fists out, eyes mad. She'd believed, really believed that her love, their family would be enough. Would mend him – and for a while, maybe it had.

'You OK, love?'

She smiled. 'Not really.'

'He'll show up.' She nodded, took in his grazed knuckles, the dark circles under his eyes. He said, 'Des'll keep looking.' And she nodded even as her heart sank.

There'd always been three people in her marriage and while she'd done her best over the years to put on a good show with Des in front of her husband, she'd never liked him. It wasn't anything she could pinpoint; a lot of the time she'd put it down to her own jealousy. No one wanted to share a spouse. But while a lot of her friends had husbands who kept a different woman in every town up and down England, Dan had never strayed in that respect.

'You look tired.'

'I am, love, cream crackered.'

'Go on up to bed. I'll tidy up down here, yeah?'

He smiled, grateful, and headed up. She listened to the familiar creak of the top step and then she opened the tallest kitchen cupboard, the one none but her ever used. She scrabbled around for the piece of paper at the back of the cupboard and stared at it. The handwriting painfully familiar and horribly unwelcome. Why she kept it she'd been unsure; today with this new awful knowledge she couldn't say she was exactly glad that she did, but she knew she needed it. She'd go first thing tomorrow and come what may she'd uncover and finally accept the truth even if it killed her.

Chapter Fifty-Seven

The door went at six in the evening.

By the time I got downstairs, Byron was sitting at the kitchen table with a man I didn't recognise.

He said, 'Grace, this is Glynn Portwell.' The policeman. And then, 'They've found River.'

I stood frozen to the spot, heart hammering. 'Is he . . .?'

'He's alive, but barely,' said the policeman.

Byron told me, 'He doesn't want this known.' Added, 'By anyone.'

'But Mae . . .'

Byron shook his head. 'Even Mae.'

The policeman said, 'Whoever did this left him for dead and until we know who it is, we want them to think they've succeeded.'

'What . . . what happened?'

'He was beaten up, very badly and left out in the woods where we found the children.'

I sat down, hand pressed to my mouth. I wondered if I was going to be sick. My mind said Des as Byron's must have, too. 'And now?'

'He's in hospital, in a coma.'

'How did you find him?'

'I've had men out on patrol around there since the boy.'
He added, 'If we'd found River even half an hour later . . .'

I sank into the chair beside Byron, sleep falling off me. I
was now brutally wide awake.

'Do you know who left him there?'

Glynn shook his head. 'No. I wish we did. I've got men
out around that area looking for any sign of who it might
have been. Whoever it was left him covered him up, which
is weird.'

Byron frowned. 'Like to hide him?'

Glynn shook his head. 'No, with a blanket like he was
being tucked in.'

'Fucking hell.' Byron looked smashed to pieces.

I took his hand and squeezed it in mine. 'He's alive, at
least.'

'Yeah,' he nodded. 'When can I see him?'

Glynn said, 'Not right now. I can't stress strongly enough
how quiet I want this kept. We've got the door to his room
at the hospital guarded but the best thing is for the culprit
to think he's succeeded.'

Byron nodded, looking up at Glynn with shiny tears in
his eyes. 'Thanks, mate.'

Glynn shrugged. 'I hope he pulls through.'

The phone rang at ten in the morning – it was Mae to tell
us they had no news their end. It took everything I had
to say, 'Same here.' Then, 'Do you need anything?' I felt
wretchedly relieved when she said no and also knew that
really, I should be going over there to see her.

Byron told me, 'I think tonight's the night.'

He'd been planning to get into the house. See how the land lay and what exactly was going on there. I said, 'I'm coming with you.'

He shook his head. 'Absolutely no way.'

I put a hand on his arm and waited for him to meet my gaze. 'Byron, I'm not asking.'

'It's probably going to be dangerous.'

'I know that.'

'If something happened to you . . .'

'I feel the same, Byron, but we are a partnership.'

He sighed but nodded agreement. I kissed him, feeling everything all at once. Love, fear, trepidation.

After he closed the door, I picked up the phone and dialled America.

'Hey.' Her voice was thick with sleep, which made me smile. I loved where I'd ended up and who with, but some days I missed our little shared room. Our chats that lasted all night and the mornings where she was like a bear with a sore head. She said, 'Have you found River?' the worry in her voice translating from there to me standing in the hallway at Byron's place. I could hear the girls clattering in the kitchen. Knew that soon Gladys would make it downstairs and we'd have a coffee and a chat. She was doing much better, and she and I had formed an easy fast friendship. Despite all the awful times the Simpsons had had, there had been a lot of fun, too, and Gladys was a natural storyteller. She wasn't cut out for motherhood, though who was made to raise four kids singlehandedly I wasn't sure, but she was managing fine now with just the girls really and no dread of financial ruin, abuse from a customer or worse.

'Yes, but Mae doesn't know and you can't tell her, or your dad.'

'I haven't spoken to either of them since I left, have I?' I'd been the one to call her with the news when River went missing, had suggested she ring Mae, but she said she couldn't handle it. She asked, 'Is he . . .?'

'He's alive. But barely and we're not allowed to see him yet.'

'Shit. Do you think it was Des?'

'It would make sense, wouldn't it?'

'We spoke just before he disappeared and he asked about it all, asked when it started.'

'What did you tell him?'

'The truth.'

I could hear her breathing at the other end of the phone, sharp gasps. She was crying. I told her, 'This isn't your fault, Lola,' for all the good it would do her.

'Will he be alright?'

'I hope so.'

'You'll make Des pay?'

'We will.'

'Good. Do you know, right up until I heard him talking to Dad about sending me away again I had hope that we'd be together.'

I didn't say anything, I just listened, a witness to her pain. 'He convinced me what we had was right, normal.'

'You were a kid, Lola. This is all on him, not you.'

'That house, I can't stop thinking about it.'

'I know, me neither.' Jacob Harse. Des Waterstone. Two men from such different walks of life. Both of them responsible for all the turmoil in mine and Lola's lives. It had to stop, and it had to stop now. I knew that as I stood there trying to console my friend that one day she'd get over this terrible thing, though how I didn't know. I'd kill Jacob if I got the chance. I knew that, had known that since the day so long ago when I'd plunged a knife between his shoulder blades. My only regret had been that my strike wasn't fatal. But I knew what Lola was thinking. What I myself was thinking. There were girls in that house just like us and they wouldn't be safe until we made sure they were.

I said, 'I'll call you again as soon as I have any news.'

Chapter Fifty-Eight

Byron was surprised to see Dan in the pub when he arrived just after opening. Dan sensed it and said, 'I'm better busy than prowling round at home, driving Mae mad.'

Byron nodded. 'No word on River?' he asked because that would be the logical question if he didn't already know.

'Nothing.' Dan shook his head. 'I'm hoping he's just gone off somewhere and got drunk or . . .' his voice trailed off. Byron imagined all of the things that were running around Dan's mind, each fear embedding in glorious technicolour. He could relate. He often went to bed at night visualising every worst-case scenario for Ben. Sometimes he dreamed about him, too, and woke in a cold sweat. Now, at least, he had Grace there. She understood him in a way no one else ever had and he knew he'd be lost without her. He wasn't happy at taking her with him tonight but he also knew she wouldn't have it any other way and he respected her and her right to make her own decisions. Going to the house would be as much about putting her past to bed as extracting justice for Lola. This, he hoped, would give her closure.

He asked Dan, 'How's Mae?' feeling a flash of guilt. He put himself in Dan's place – the man had a right to know.

About Lola, yes, but also about his son. What if he didn't make it and Dan hadn't had a chance to visit, or Mae.

He was just about to open his mouth when the door to the pub swung open and Des walked in. Dan's face lit up, all of the anxiety of a moment ago wiped clean. Byron took the scene in and thanked God for Des's arrival. There was no room for softness in this. This was bigger than him and Grace, bigger than Mae and Dan. There were kids in that house. From what Byron had gleaned from poor Betty that woman was out recruiting every few months, which meant either there were loads of them or they often needed replacing. He felt sick just thinking about it and any reservations he had were pushed to one side.

Des slapped him on the shoulder. 'Alright, boy?' Byron was taller than Des and smarter, but Des was still higher in his status. Not for long, though, and it was that thought that enabled Byron to crack a wide smile and say, 'Yeah, OK,' though inside his guts were churning.

Chapter Fifty-Nine

Mae's heart was heavy as she walked down familiar streets, like a leaden ball burning in the centre of her chest. Everything felt heavy. The buggy that she pushed ahead of her, her precious grandson seated within. The product of rape because even if Lola had said yes, you couldn't extract consent from a child. Her hands on the handlebars, her limbs. She'd taken a sleeping tablet last night. Had needed to, to stop her spending the night brutally wide awake pacing the length of the house. To stop her screaming like a lunatic, at her husband, herself. Des. She wasn't sure who she was angriest at, but she could feel it, eating into her, taking nibbles from all the good bits. A rage so big and reckless she was scared of the day it was let loose and scared, too, that that day was almost upon her.

Marriage was all about compromise. A series of shifting yourself and your needs around to suit the other person. Then persons, when kids came along. Mae had done that from such a young age she didn't often think about her needs or wants. If you'd have asked her two years ago she'd have said she had everything. A perfect life. Handsome, rich husband. Healthy, happy kids. Even when Lola had fallen Mae had been OK. Thought her family were fine.

Not ideal that her daughter found herself in the family way at just fifteen and worse still that she wouldn't name the lad. But even that, Mae had understood. She loved her husband but she wasn't blind to his flaws and she could see things from Lola's perspective. Dan was a lunatic when the mood took him and if she'd given up the boy's name he'd be in trouble. Mae had also run over the possibility that her daughter wasn't that into the guy and therefore didn't want to be forced into a marriage she wasn't happy in. Mae didn't even begrudge her that. Things were different now for girls as the seventies approached. You didn't have to just grow up, get a fella, have kids. Look at young Grace who'd never have her own but ran the shop far better than Dan or River ever had.

She was at the front door standing before the austere set of concrete steps she'd climbed so many times before that she could conjure up the feel of them before she'd put her foot on them. The smell was pungent, carbolic soap the odour of her childhood, and it hit her now. As it was she didn't get a chance to step up. The door swung open.

Mae stared into eyes so similar to her own.

'Hello, Mum.'

Sophia Collins looked at her daughter, took in the pram in her hands and swung the door open with a sigh. 'I suppose you'd better come in then.'

Mae took Sam out and he wobbled on her hip. Sophia reached out and caught his hand, smiling at the boy who grinned right back. 'Yours?'

'My Lola's.'

'Ah.'

'Mine for all intents and purposes though.' And then, 'I wouldn't turn one of my own away.' Watched her mother wince as the words landed where they were aimed and stung. She felt immediate regret but was unable to take the words back, even considering the reason she was there.

Mae put Sam on the floor and looked around. It had changed since she was last there, which must have been close to twenty years ago. Sophia swooped into the kitchen and Mae heard familiar sounds. The kettle whistling, a biscuit tin lid popping open. Her heart felt a stab of pain. Saying goodbye to her mother and father, her brother was the hardest thing Mae had ever done but, until this day, she'd never regretted her choice. Had been so sure of her husband, their marriage. Had she though? She'd taken over care of the kids when they were young, yes, but she'd never let River out of her sight, had never really left him and Dan alone together, not until Lola. Ironic when it wasn't him who'd needed watching in the end. She felt a swell of sadness just thinking about her son. He always came home. No matter what. He'd been gone for two days. She hadn't given up hope he'd be found alive though. Couldn't give that up.

Sophia was back with a tray. Mugs of tea were balanced on it and a plate of biscuits. She set it down. Handed a cup to Mae who took it, gratefully wrapping her hands around its warmth. Glad to have something to do with her hands lest they started wringing in the air.

Sophia gave Sam a biscuit and the boy took it with a grin. Sophia smiled back. 'Handsome thing, isn't he?'

Mae nodded. 'A lovely nature, too.'

'Well then. That's good, eh?'

The tears came then, unexpected. Sophia walked across the room, sat next to her estranged daughter on the sofa and took her in her arms. She'd always known this day would come. Truth would out, it was always the way. People – they were only as sick as their secrets after all, and sickness had a way of bleeding into others even when you didn't want that to be the case.

She murmured things to Mae, stroked her hair, strands of it, she noted, turning grey now. It had been that long. She didn't look so different other than that, mind. Sophia understood she and Dan had money these days, that the kids were well provided for. She'd tried to console herself with that over the years, pushing back darker worries, hoping against hope that the little ones would be safe. That somewhere in her heart, hidden in layers of denial, Mae knew the truth and would protect them.

Chapter Sixty

Emma had a stash. She'd been saving the little white tablets that Nina gave her. It had been hard because those tablets guaranteed her lovely, wonderful blankness for anywhere up to twelve hours. Without them, she hardly slept at all. But she couldn't bear the thought of her or Ben going like Martha or Jackson. Now she had the added burden of being worried about the new girl. She didn't want to care, tried to make herself hard inside so she didn't have to, but it didn't work. It was her cross to bear, she knew that. A sweet, sensitive nature. She wouldn't have survived a week in here; it was the other children who'd got her through, given her a reason to keep on keeping on.

For them, not her.

The day had faded away and outside it was dark and raining. The door to her bedroom swung open. Nina. Her tall body cast a shadow in the lamp-lit room. Emma looked at her blankly. Nina smiled her horrible smile. Emma had been charmed by it once, but now she could see her mistake, remembered Betty's words of warning, 'If something seems too good to be true, it probably is.'

The lesson had been learnt too late for Emma. Too late for Ben.

'You need to start getting ready, we have a new group arriving shortly. You'll be in charge of the girls. One hour and I'll introduce you.'

Group? In charge of the girls? Did this mean there were more boys, too? Emma ran her hand along the side of her mattress, felt for the crumpled bit of tissue, counted the pills again. Enough for her and Ben, but what about the others? She couldn't worry about them, she decided. She didn't have the room or capacity for it.

She stood, stretched her body, dimly registering the various aches and pains it had most mornings. She ran a bath and prayed that God would forgive her for taking her life and Ben's, that he was a kind, forgiving being and not the hellish nightmare of Sunday schools. Surely if there was any goodness, they might be allowed some peace in death.

Chapter Sixty-One

Glynn felt strange being here, again, at Byron's house. And weirder still that none of his colleagues knew where he was or what was about to happen with his knowledge. Ironic really that this nefarious thing would, hopefully, free him from any future skulduggery. That's all he wanted, a fresh start or more precisely, to go back to how it had been. There was no way that he'd be able to get a warrant to enter the premises of that doomed, beautiful mansion in Mayfair. It was laughable that a job they should have been doing would fall to criminals. He didn't think of Byron that way, though. Byron wasn't unlike him in a lot of respects. He'd ended up where he was through necessity rather than desire. He wasn't like the Dans and Deses of the world and Glynn knew the lad would go on to have great success; and after meeting Grace, whom he immediately warmed to, he could see they would be a formidable couple.

'Repeat back to me what will happen, Glynn.' Byron had a frown of concentration on his face.

'I'll be here watching to see where Harse is, you'll be at the Anchor.'

Byron nodded – he'd squared it with the landlord there who was expecting him and Grace and had been paid handsomely for his troubles. 'When I see Harse is near, I'll call you at the pub.'

'Right.'

A pause, then Glynn asked, 'What are you going to do?'

Byron kept his gaze level. 'Whatever we need to.' Glynn took in the steely glint in the young man's eye and looked at Grace, who appeared just as determined.

Byron added, 'You're best not asking questions, Glynn. Trust me when I say it will be worth it. For all of us.'

Byron picked up the Salomi brothers en route. Made swift introductions to Grace. Timmy said, 'You'll be OK, will you?'

She smiled. 'I'll be fine, thanks, will you?'

Tim laughed his bellowing laugh and clapped Byron on the shoulder. 'She's a keeper, mate.'

Byron rolled his eyes at Grace who smiled back. Men weren't used to women like her, she understood that. She also understood that her experiences had shaped her, brought her to this point. She was strong and determined but once this day was done, she'd go and live the life of a civilian. Not quite the one she'd been born for, that evaporated the day her father died, but a decent life, nonetheless. She thought often of her daughter and she'd keep checking in, making sure she was OK, but she wouldn't disrupt the girl's life.

The Salomis would take out Des. They would leave Dan alone unless they had to. She and Byron were both hopeful, though, that Dan would let things go quietly once it was just him, see sense and take what he'd earned and settle down. He and Mae had Sam to raise, money in the bank and hopefully they'd still have River to think about, too. Maybe they'd go to Hollywood, maybe by the time they got there Lola would be a star.

Either way, neither Grace nor Byron felt bad about Des. He was a sick fuck who needed taking out. But both were nervous about what the night ahead would involve.

Chapter Sixty-Two

Sophia watched Mae playing with the little one. She'd been a good mother, she imagined. Wasn't surprised by it. She'd always been caring and clever, and rebellious. When she'd first brought Dan home she and Mick, God rest his soul, had had their reservations, of course. Everyone knew how he and Des Waterstone made their money but no one could entirely blame them either. The post-war years had seen plenty of families in London ravaged. Her own husband had been traumatised by the action he'd seen over there, and plenty never saw men come home. People were poor before the boom began. Really devastatingly poor. Dan and Des both came from those families and had been shunted into children's homes when they should have been blessed by a mother's love.

No, the criminality, the ducking and diving, her and Mick could have swallowed and would have, too. They were good parents. Dedicated and loving. They had Mae, the eldest and her brother, Mick Junior, eight years later. An unexpected blessing they hadn't anticipated at all as there had been some complications with Mae that made it seem unlikely. But there he was, a sweet bonny child, a welcome addition to their family.

'You've enjoyed raising them, Mae?'

She nodded. 'Loved it, am glad to have him for my later years.'

Sophia nodded. 'You should be. A sweet little thing.' A pause and then, 'He has the look of your brother.'

Mae nodded. She'd seen it as soon as Lola had got him home. He had dark colouring, like Des, though she pushed that thought away every time it came to her. Just a thought but one that was laughing in her face. How did she not know? Why hadn't she seen what was unfolding before her very eyes? Sophia stood, took a photo from the mantelpiece and handed it to her daughter. Mae's eyes filled with tears. She ran a hand along his face; they had their arms around each other and were grinning like they hadn't a care in the world, which she supposed was true.

'How is he?'

'He's doing alright.' Sophia added, 'Now.'

'Married?'

Sophia shook her head. 'That sort of thing was ruined for him.'

The tears fell then before she could stop them. 'He used to lie all the time, Mum.'

Sophia nodded and felt sad for her daughter in that moment. 'He did, yes. Exaggerated things anyway.' She grinned. 'A natural born bullshitter, your dad always called him. It's what he does for a living now, you know.'

Mae frowned. 'Is it?'

'Yes. Writes children's stories, under a different name. Loves it, too, and they sell quite well.'

'Oh.' She wished she'd known that, imagined he would

have been a fantastic uncle. Someone to come over and read to them. Both of hers had devoured books growing up. She wondered if she'd read any of her brother's to them and feels a terrible rush of shame that she wouldn't have even known.

'Come on, child,' Sophia said. 'Spill your troubles and let's see what we can do.'

Chapter Sixty-Three

My heart beat a tattoo in my chest, I was a wretched bag of nerves. The pub was almost empty and I was relieved. Byron and I drew stares, and often abuse, all the time and coupled with the Salomi brothers we were not an inconspicuous party. There was nothing to do other than wait it out, which we did.

We were all on edge, but the Salomi brothers kept up a stream of light-hearted banter. I found I liked them and knew that their acquaintance would benefit us in the future.

When the phone went, we all jumped.

Byron took the call. We'd agreed he and I would go in first, leaving the gate open for the brothers to follow if we weren't back in half an hour. We had two guns. Byron had one and Tim had the other. Byron put the phone down, came out and nodded to me.

The pub was on the corner of the private road which had the large house at its end. We crept along, keeping close to the high wall which surrounded it. In the air was the faint scent of lavender and roses. I imagined behind that wall were beautiful grounds, a flourishing garden in the middle of the city hiding a festering and terrible secret.

There was a tall, curved ledge at the side of the gate and we put ourselves behind it then. Dressed head to toe in black and super aware of every movement, every breath. I could feel Byron's warm breath on the top of my head. I clung to him then, arms wrapped around his waist, but my senses alert for the car. I didn't want to lose him. I didn't want to die. This task, though, would make both of those things possible. Likely, even. But we had the same goal even if we held it for different reasons. We were tighter and those reasons by then had become mingled so that I wanted the best for him, and he for me. He wanted his chance in the world. And his chance would be ours. Getting rid of Des and a pay-out from the Salomis made that possible. I wanted some sort of rough justice for me and for Chloe. She was thriving and I was glad of it, but she'd never know her real mother and that had to be paid for somehow, along with my own heartbreak and the barren broken womb he'd left me with.

Finally, we both knew we had to free the children who were there. I didn't know then what the outcome of that would be but Byron said Glynn would help with anything official, and I'd found I liked and trusted the policeman that Dan had kept a moral and financial prisoner for years now.

We heard the sound of a car approaching. A man got out. *It's him*, I thought, and it took all my will and strength not to make a run for him now, grab the gun, shoot him down. We heard the gate clank slowly open, waited ten seconds after hearing him drive in and slipped inside the grounds.

Byron removed a long metal pipe from his bag and wedged it between the two gates, leaving enough room for the brothers to get through.

Chapter Sixty-Four

Sophia shook her head as Mae finished speaking, filling her mother in on all that had happened and where she was at now. She said to her daughter. 'I'm so sorry, love.'

'I should have believed him.' Sophia wasn't going to argue with that. Those words took her back twenty years when she'd begged her daughter to listen to her, listen to Mick and her father. Dan had abused Mick Junior. For years, by the time it all came to light. He was sick, wrong. Sophia had known immediately Mick Junior was telling the truth. Hadn't doubted him for a second. And everything had made sense to her then. The way he'd changed and Sophia's own feelings towards Dan, which was that, skulduggery aside, he was just too good to be true. A polished act, so polished, so believable that Mae had believed him over her own brother. Chosen him over her own family.

Dan was her love and Sophia got it – she was under his spell, and she could see why. He was so handsome, so charming. So broken.

She didn't know what had happened to him or Des in those homes, though she had her suspicions, but she knew plenty of other people who'd been dragged up in them and hadn't turned into awful predators like her unwanted son-in-law. Dan and Mick Junior had got along so well. Sophia and Mick Senior had been delighted, said to each other, what a wonderful father he'd make one day. She herself had admired him then, been happy to have her misgivings proven wrong. A man who'd overcome terrible odds. And it was clear as day that he was head over heels in love with their Mae.

She remembered the change in Mick Junior. He'd started wetting the bed, having trouble sleeping. There were bruises on his little body that were unaccounted for. Eventually he'd told his mother the truth, and Sophia had seen that was what it was as the poor boy spoke.

Devastating. For their whole family and she felt for her daughter. God knows you wouldn't want to believe it of the first man you'd fallen for, the one who was going to give you a good life.

'You loved Dan.'

'I still do, Mum, but if Des is up to this sort of thing and they are still so close . . .'

Sophia sighed and sat next to her daughter, arm around her shoulders. 'You think they'd each know the other's secrets?'

Mae nodded. 'I do, yeah, and I think Dan's loyalty will always be with him over us.' She looked at her mother then. 'I think Des might have killed River.' She clamped a hand to her mouth as soon as the words were out. They'd been spinning round and around in her mind all day and now she'd said them, she could never, ever take them back.

Sophia said, 'Then you'll need to do something about it, Mae.'

'I know.'

'What will it be, Mae?'

Mae stood, resolve pushing her to her feet. She knew exactly what had to be done. Her heartbreak was nothing compared to her children's. 'Can you look after him for me? Maybe even overnight?'

Sophia beamed. 'Oh, I'd love to.'

'Your great-grandson.' Sophia picked him up, felt the plump heft of him. The third generation of hers, she'd missed the one between him and Mae.

Mae said, 'You'll love Lola.' She didn't add River as she couldn't bear to entertain any possibility of him being alive. The hope would kill her, though she'd not fully accepted his death yet either. This limbo was preferable for now. Now she had a job to do, and do it she would.

Chapter Sixty-Five

The blond man was there. J. Pawing at her. Each time his hands touched her flesh she felt a swell of nausea and had to fight the urge to slap his hands off and away. She had the pills, she had a way out. Nina had said the new children would arrive the following day but for tonight she and the new girl were the entertainment. The big man was there as he usually was in the evenings now. Emma heard him and Nina talking and laughing as though everything was fine. She knew he'd taken the new girl last night and she'd looked awful this morning. Now she was washed, made up and pretty but for the vacant glassy look in her eyes. If Emma had to guess she figured the girl was still taking her pills.

The blond man stood and stretched his hand out to her. She took it, her heart heavy. She'd asked him for help. So stupid was she. And Martha was dead now because of it. Because of her.

They went into one of the bedrooms, the same one he always chose. She was his favourite, and he liked to keep up the pretence that theirs was a real relationship rather than a terrible transaction which she got nothing out of. But Nina had mentioned more than once that she was becoming too mature for him. Her body was changing, that was for sure. She still had to take a pill every day so there were no babies and now, she imagined there was cause for her to. Nina said the day she came on that it was a shame, she'd been hoping for a few more years out of her. Emma hated her so much.

She lay back on the bed, eyes closed, mind willing itself to be away, somewhere far, far away. Not to a better time because in her young life she hadn't really known any of those, so to someone else's life then. She tried to tune out the grunting sounds he made above her.

She lay next to him, listening to his laboured, fast breathing start to even out.

Once she was sure he was asleep, she stood, went to her bedroom, got the pills. She headed into the kitchen, smashed them to pulp on a wooden chopping board where Nina cut meat and vegetables. She poured two glasses of juice, emptying the powder into them, then headed upstairs, resting one glass on the floor as she opened the door to Ben's room, picking it up again as she walked in.

The little boy sat up, grinning at her and she felt her heart ache. He deserved so much better than what he'd had.

Life wasn't fair but this felt like the worst thing of all.

She forced a smile and told him, 'I brought you a drink.

Chapter Sixty-Six

'That you, love?'

Mae's heart felt like it might smash to pieces at the familiar sound of his voice and the cheeriness of his greeting. How many years had that voice been her beacon? A homing call wherever she was. When she was a little girl, she used to watch her parents. To see the comfort they took from one another, the companionship and teamwork that was the foundation of her life. She'd known that was what she wanted, that she wouldn't settle for anything less. Who knew that when she found it, it would end up here, like this? Her father had died ten years ago. She only knew because her mother sent a card, the one she'd looked at before walking over to her house. Opening the door to her painful past. Even then she'd been too stubborn to go home. Too scared, more like. She had felt angry with them, especially her brother, and she was right when she said to Sophia that he was always telling lies. He had been, back then – the boy who cried wolf. Not that time, though, and now she knew it, had had an inkling of it then but pushed it away. Dan was kind, caring. She couldn't reconcile the man she shared a bed with, the only man she'd ever shared a bed with, with someone who abused little boys. Who had

286

abused her brother. If Des had been at it with Lola, that meant he thought he'd get away with it no matter what. She wasn't sure if Dan knew about Lo specifically but she was fairly certain that some of the pictures River had found and taken to Byron and Grace were Dan's not Des's so maybe he had known. She didn't suppose it mattered anymore. Des was what he was, Dan was what he was. Her life, her marriage, their relationship as man and woman was an illusion. One she'd bought into young. She'd wanted to. He made her happy. That was the truth of it. And if he could make her so happy that meant he couldn't be a monster. Only it didn't and he was.

She unwound her scarf, pulled off her mittens and hung her coat. Everything she'd done a million times before, but it all felt like the last time. A finality. She knew that after today nothing could ever be the same again. She walked into the sitting room and smiled softly at Dan who gave her a wary grin back and said, 'Still no sign, love. I'm so sorry.'

'Thanks for looking.' She wondered where he'd been really, and where was Des?

'Cuppa?'

He nodded. 'Please.' Then, 'Where's the little man?'

'Over with Gladys and the girls, just for a night. I'm shattered.'

'Understandable, love. And besides, having the house to ourselves might not be such a bad thing.' He waggled his eyebrows at her and she forced herself to smile back. 'Maybe so.'

He was always so eager for her, always ready to jump

into bed. Even in a crisis. It was one of the aspects of their relationship she'd used in her own mind to discredit what her brother had said to their mum. It couldn't be true or they wouldn't have the physical relationship they did, would they? She hadn't recognised the monstrous version of her husband depicted by Mick Junior.

She hadn't wanted to. That was the sad truth.

As she'd got older, wiser, she'd thought about it a few times. Not least over holiday seasons or on the kids' birthdays. They'd have been brilliant grandparents, her mum and dad, but hadn't been given that chance.

Because of her.

Because of the man sitting in the front room, waiting for his cup of tea.

She boiled it as usual, adding the crushed sleeping tablets and an extra spoon of sugar that she hoped would disguise the taste. She handed him the mug, kicked off her shoes and curled up in the armchair next to his, listening to him slurp at the drink and waiting.

Chapter Sixty-Seven

Jacob Harse was lying on his back, snoring softly, a sheet draped across his naked body. Grace went and sat on the edge of the bed, watching him fascinated. In her mind he was so much bigger than this, larger than life. Here he lay though, small, pathetic, diminished. She leant forward and his eyes snapped open, looking straight at her. He frowned. 'Who the devil are you?' And she swiped out, bringing the knife across his throat. Blood sprang up in glistening drops but it was just a long thin scratch, not deep enough for real damage, she realised as he carried on breathing, hand reaching for his throat, and even that act of violence felt awful and wrong to her. She'd been numb last time when she'd stabbed him, walking away calm and collected. Numb with her grief for Chloe, but it wasn't who she was. Not really. She dropped the knife. Stood up, backing away from him now. He was clutching at his neck, but sat up. Blood dripped down across his bare chest. 'Who?' he said, his voice strangled.

'Nora's girl.'

Recognition dawned and along with it fear, then he sank down, like an inflatable losing air, and his eyes rolled back in his head. He was unconscious but his hard gargling breath was loud and clear. Grace walked away from him, heading out of the room, her breath ragged and sharp.

Byron looked up as she stepped back out into the hallway. Her eyes were fiery and ablaze. 'He's still alive.' Her voice was nearly a whisper. Byron hadn't wanted this for her, would have preferred she'd left it to him, but he could understand her need. The motivation. He said, 'Is he conscious?'

She nodded. Byron took that in, and he was glad that the man hadn't died yet, that his Grace wasn't a killer. Killing was no good for the soul. He knew that and he didn't wish it upon her.

'He'll go to prison for this, it'll make the papers.'

Grace nodded.

Byron said, 'Find any kids?'

'Not yet.'

He took her hand in his and squeezed it. 'Come on then.'

Grace went ahead of Byron, checking rooms on the right while he took the left. They were upstairs but in what appeared to be a separate wing to where they'd left Jacob. Byron had stopped in an office and was glancing over files and paperwork. Grace opened a door at the end of the hall and saw a little girl holding two glasses and a boy sitting up in bed, hair messy and in pyjamas. Both looked at her in surprise. The girl was so startled she dropped the tumblers, which fell to the carpeted floor, landing silently, their contents immediately staining the plush cream shag pile. The girl made a sort of cry, clamping a hand to her mouth, stepping protectively in front of the little lad. Grace said, 'It's OK. We're here to help you. Nod if you can keep quiet.'

She nodded. Grace smiled at her and pressed a finger to her lips. 'Talk quietly, but tell me if you know where Des is.'

She frowned. 'The big man?'

'Dark hair, scar over his eye?'

'Downstairs with Nina.'

'Stay here. Keep him safe. We'll come back for you.'

The girl said, 'There's another girl, down the hall.'

'Can you get her?'

'I don't think so, she's in with the judge.'

Byron stepped in and Grace turned to look at him, open-mouthed and wide-eyed.

'Byron?' she frowned. But he stepped forward past her, past the girl. The little boy got out of the bed and stood in front of him, grinning. 'I knew you'd come.'

Grace watched the two of them in fascination as the realisation dawned on her.

She looked at the girl who was also watching them, transfixed, and said, 'Byron is Ben's big brother.'

He was clinging to him now and the boy had his arms wrapped around his neck. Byron pulled back, looking at his face. Taking in every detail.

'Ben,' he managed.

Ben grinned.

'Are you . . .? What happened?'

'That Dan Scott-Tyler.'

Byron frowned. 'What?' His heart was hammering.

'He was always nice to me, By, but he started buying me sweets, stuff like that, taking me on walks.'

'Why didn't you say?'

'Didn't think to, thought he was just being nice.'

'What changed?'

'He asked me to do something.'

Byron swallowed, saliva skimming over a thick lump in his throat.

Ben shook his head. 'No, I never, and he tried to laugh it off, make out he was joking and said I shouldn't tell anyone. I said I wouldn't, but I would, Byron, I'd have told you.' He shrugged, his little shoulders rising up and down in thin pyjamas. 'I think he knew it, too. Big Des came out to the park where we were. I said I'd walk home, was fine. But Dan said he insisted, then brought me here.'

'Oh God, Ben, I'm so sorry.'

Ben said, 'It's OK. You came, I knew you would. Didn't I say, Emma?' The girl looked stunned. Grace was shocked. Dan was as bad as Des. Two sides of the same coin. Byron looked at her and she could see her own shock reflected on his face.

Byron turned to the girl. 'Grace, you get them out, OK?'

She nodded.

He said to the girl, 'Where are the grown-ups?'

'Downstairs.' Her voice was hardly a whisper.

Des and a woman were sitting at a kitchen table. Des stood up, looking at Byron in surprise. 'What the hell are you doing here?'

'I know what you are, and I know about Dan.' The full force of his anger pushed the words out. Des held up his hands. 'Look, the thing with Ben was a mistake. Dan was sorry about it.'

'Sorry?' Byron's voice was loud and incredulous. Nina

292

looked from one to the other, sensing the tense danger in the air.

Des said, 'We're not bad people,' in a voice so calm that Byron realised he actually believed it.

'They are children.'

Des shrugged. 'Most of them come through here have been through far worse already.'

'Oh, what, you're offering them a decent home?'

Des shrugged. 'They are fed. Clothed. They've got no one out there that misses them.'

'Ben did.'

'Like I said, a mistake.'

Byron moved forward, grabbing Des and manoeuvring himself behind him. Des made to turn around – he was bigger than Byron, but Byron was younger, full of rage and kept him held close. He took out a knife quickly and, with no fuss, slashed a long, deep cut across the man's throat at the table where he had sat, cocky as ever. He'd worked alongside him, drunk with him even but he'd never liked him, and he liked what he did even less.

The woman made to stand up, mouth open like she was about to shout.

Byron grabbed her from behind, pulled the set of hand-cuffs from his pocket and locked her to the chair she sat in. She started to open her mouth again and he gagged her.

Chapter Sixty-Eight

I literally bumped into the Salomi brothers as I fled that awful place, the boy and a girl gripping each of my hands. Tim paused. 'OK?'

I nodded, still too shaken up to speak.

'Big Des?'

'Gone,' I told him and Tim grinned.

'Byron?'

'On his way.'

'Get in the car. Mason and I will wait for Byron, and we can walk back, OK?'

I nodded. Ran to the car, getting the children in. The girl said, 'The other girl?'

'The police will be coming, OK?'

'What about us?'

'You'll come with us for now.'

She nodded. Her eyes had dark rings. Both children looked well-fed. The girl was in a long dress now, preferable to the too-old lingerie she'd been in when we'd found her. I thought back to my own awful experience with that same man. She must have just left the room where I'd found him moments before I arrived. I'd have been not much older than she was, I suspected. I reached back, took her hand.

'It'll be OK,' I promised, desperately hoping that would be true.

The car door opened, and I almost jumped out of my skin. He got in fast, turned the key and we were off.

I said to him, 'Byron, I thought we were coming back for you?'

'I had to get out, thought I'd come find you. The police are on their way. Where to?'

'Our place. They need food and rest.'

'Ben, I'm taking you home,' said Byron, his voice a strangled cry. Not only had we literally fought my demon and secured our future, we'd also unknowingly rescued his little brother, too.

Chapter Sixty-Nine

'I feel a bit off, love.'

Mae smiled at him. He looked at her, pupils wide, eyes glassy. 'Are you alright?'

'I need a glass of water.' He attempted to stand and slid forward, his knees hitting the carpet.

She went to him, helped him back into the chair. 'I'll get it.'

She came back, helped him hold the glass. He was shaky, she saw, and his skin had a horrible grey tinge. Sweat worked down his brow, small droplets of it resting on his upper lip. He sipped noisily. Sank back into the chair. She put the glass on the table next to her, sat back where she had been watching him, years of memories floating across her mind. Such happy ones, too. She'd been so happy, at times wondering what she'd done to deserve such a great life. Always, though, in the background that voice had whispered. She'd kept a close eye on River. Always careful, making sure she was the last to go to bed, the first one up. She was relieved when he made it into his late teenage years. She hadn't thought to watch Lola, though she should have.

'Penny for them?' Dan's voice was thin and raspy.

'I was thinking that although Sam has Des's colouring, he doesn't have his features, nor his temperament.'

Dan frowned. The sweat was cascading now. He leaned forward, one hand across his gut. 'What are you talking about?'

'Des. He's Sam's dad.'

Dan frowned, face aghast.

'Oh, you didn't know then?'

''Course I didn't fucking know.' He went to get up, slumped back down again. 'My best fucking mate.'

'River found some photos,' Byron said.'

His eyes shifted, even in the midst of the obvious discomfort being wrought on his body. She imagined organs were starting to shut down, perhaps his heart was speeding up. She wasn't sure what it looked like to be honest, an overdose.

'What pictures?' But there was a weakness in the question. She knew it and he knew it, too.

'Little Mick wasn't lying that time, was he?'

A silence. Dan's face was panicked, sad. A deer caught in headlights. 'I've spent a lifetime, Mae, trying to make it up to you. I've been a good husband, haven't I?'

She nodded. 'You have, yeah.'

'Then this,' he waved his hand around, 'thing.'

She reached to the table next to her, picked up the half-full glass, stood and threw it at the wall. Shards of it rained down around her husband like twinkling rain. 'This thing. This fucking thing?'

He put his hands up as some sort of protection, but it was useless. He was dead already. Even if she rang for an ambulance now, which she wasn't going to do, she doubted he'd make it.

He reached for her as she stood before him, trembling with her own rage. At him, herself. She wasn't sure. She'd had a glimmer of worry when Ben disappeared. She'd seen Dan talking to him out on their road. But Dan talked to everyone. Men, women, children. It was part of his appeal. The gangster with a heart. Your regular everyman. If she'd been fooled, why wouldn't everyone else be? She hadn't pushed it and figured if he'd had anything to do with it, he certainly wouldn't have taken Byron on. Only a monster would do that.

Which was exactly what he was.

She turned and walked from the room, out into their little garden. She could hear him, inside, limbs heavy now and unable to move, calling her name. She felt a sweet and bitter relief as the cries got quieter and eventually when they stopped, she allowed herself the tears she knew she had to shed. Grief for her, her daughter. Her brother, her son. Her family.

Chapter Seventy

The judge and Jacob Harse made headlines. He'd survived his injury again. The second time I'd shunted a blade into him, neither attack fatal. His wife and children had fled to her parents in the countryside. I considered that we'd done them a favour. Both would go to prison for a long time, as would Nina who was currently the prime suspect in Des Waterstone's murder, too. The Salomis paid out. Byron and I opened a casino in Mayfair, the first of many. River made a slow but full recovery. He managed all our key accounts, flying out to meet investors and looking at ways to expand. He was charming, loveable and good at his job, which took him around the world. He married a girl who worked in a shop on the Portobello Road, Cindy, and they had three children who Mae and her mother, Sophia, doted upon. Her brother Mick, it turned out, was a brilliant uncle to River's children and to Sam. On the opening night of our first casino, Lola came over to sing. She drew crowds, a name now in all those papers, having landed her first feature film. She was on husband number three but her best friend in the world was her manager and, I thought, for her, perhaps that platonic relationship would be the one that defined her life. At least it wasn't Des. Byron and I had not moved into a place of our own, but we had bought a bigger house. In it was his mother, still pissed, but mollycoddled by the rest of us, his sisters and Vanessa, who was our housekeeper, Emma and Ben. Emma and I had formed a very close friendship. She and Ben were back in school and, I hoped, on the mend or as much as they ever could be. She was a bright girl and we had money, which would hopefully ease her future. Mae hadn't been the same exactly, but I'm glad to say all the good things about her remained so, even if she had a harder glint in her eye than she used to. Dan's death was ruled as a suicide. Videos from the house of horrors had been found when Glynn and his team swept in. Dan and Des were featured in plenty of them so that was a good enough reason, according to Glynn. The smashed glass was difficult to explain. Mae said the grief of finding him had overwhelmed her and no one who could make a difference pushed at it.

My daughter, Chloe, was doing well.

One day, Byron and I walked by the house she lived in and there she was, a little girl now, tightening the handlebars of her bike on the drive. A tall man with sandy hair was helping her. She smiled when we passed and I raised my hand to her and the man, her father, far better for the job than her biological one, waved back.

That was all I would have of her. All it felt OK to take and I've made my peace there. As much as I could anyway.

You had to count your blessings really and mine were plentiful.

Acknowledgements

Thanks to my agent Hattie Grunewald for your invaluable input, as always. Thank you to everyone at Orion who has worked on this book, in particular Rhea Kurien for her keen editorial eye and Sanah Ahmed for an array of administrative duties and far more beyond, I'm sure. Thanks also to Sally Partington who did a truly excellent job proof reading *Taken* and made the final stage of edits very enjoyable.

Thanks to my husband and sons for everything, not least for making it through long and awful lockdowns where I wrote at funny hours, 'home schooled' two of you terribly and was likely more short tempered than normal. I'd be lost without you, likewise the brilliant friends I'm blessed with.

Credits

Niki Mackay and Orion Fiction would like to thank everyone at Orion who worked on the publication of *Taken* in the UK.

Editorial
Rhea Kurien
Sanah Ahmed

Copyeditor
Amanda Rutter

Proofreader
Sally Partington

Contracts
Anne Goddard
Humayra Ahmed
Ellie Bowker

Audio
Paul Stark
Jake Alderson

Operations
Jo Jacobs
Sharon Willis

Editorial Management
Charlie Panayiotou
Jane Hughes
Bartley Shaw
Tamara Morriss

Finance
Jasdip Nandra
Afeera Ahmed
Elizabeth Beaumont
Sue Baker

Production
Ruth Sharvell

Sales
Jen Wilson
Esther Waters
Victoria Laws
Rachael Hum
Anna Egelstaff
Frances Doyle
Georgina Cutler

Design
Charlotte Abrams-Simpson
Joanna Ridley
Nick May

'Psychological suspense at its best'
VICTORIA SELMAN

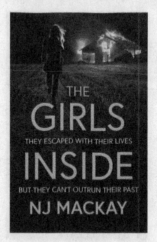

Blue grew up in the Black House.

In remotest Wales, Joseph Carillo recruited young, lonely women to join his community and adopt his erratic views. Blue's mother was one of them. But when the Black House goes up in flames, Blue escapes to freedom and never stops running.

Twenty years later, when Blue's old dormmate commits suicide, Blue receives a strange call. She has been awarded sole custody of Natasha's daughter. But things don't add up. The girls haven't spoken since the night of the fire.

As Blue begins to dig into Natasha's life, her suspicions take her all the way back to that fateful night . . . But will the truth help Blue to face her past, or will it put everyone she holds close in danger?

Available in eBook now!

Don't miss P.I. Madison Attallee's heart-racing cases:

They say I'm a murderer.
Six years ago, Kate Reynolds was found
holding the body of her best friend.

I plead guilty.
Kate has been in prison ever since, but
now her sentence is up.

But the truth is, I didn't do it.
There's only one person who can help:
Private Investigator Madison Attallee, the
first officer on the scene all those years ago.

But there's someone out there who doesn't
want Kate digging up the past. Someone
who is willing to keep the truth buried at
any cost.

Last night I betrayed my husband.
This morning my daughter disappeared.
My husband may have forgiven my
first mistake.
But he will never forget this.
And so I have to find her.
Before it's too late. For all of us.

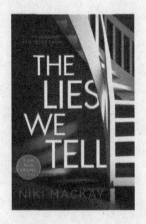

**Both available in paperback,
audio and eBook now!**